"YOU MAKE ME TALK TOO MUCH," COOPER murmured, running his thumb along the curve of her cheek.

Jessica felt the change in him, felt the tension in him escalate, moving another degree to the edge. He was unpredictable and dangerous. He was off-limits. Any fool could see it, and she wasn't a fool.

"I'm sorry," she whispered, her gaze locked with his.

"I don't want your sympathy. I want your kiss." His hand slid to the back of her neck and his mouth lowered to hers.

He'd taken away the excuse of surprise. She'd known he was going to kiss her, and she hadn't made a move to stop him. Worse, when his lips touched hers and parted, she instinctively did the same.

As he deepened the kiss, Jessica felt her knees weaken. Cooper caught her with his arm around her back, drawing her closer and more intimately into the embrace.

No battle raged in her heart, no thought of retreat crossed her mind. He tasted of wine and brought pleasure, infused her senses and lit a flame of long-lost desire in her core. When his hand glided down the length of her back and molded her to his body, she surrendered. . . .

## WHAT ARE *LOVESWEPT* ROMANCES?

*They are stories of true romance and touching emotion. We believe those two very important ingredients are constants in our highly sensual and very believable stories in the LOVESWEPT line. Our goal is to give you, the reader, stories of consistently high quality that may sometimes make you laugh, sometimes make you cry, but are always fresh and creative and contain many delightful surprises within their pages.*

*Most romance fans read an enormous number of books. Those they truly love, they keep. Others may be traded with friends and soon forgotten. We hope that each LOVESWEPT romance will be a treasure—a "keeper." We will always try to publish*

## LOVE STORIES YOU'LL NEVER FORGET BY AUTHORS YOU'LL ALWAYS REMEMBER

*The Editors*

# THE DRAGON
# AND
# THE DOVE

## GLENNA
## McREYNOLDS

BANTAM BOOKS
NEW YORK · TORONTO · LONDON · SYDNEY · AUCKLAND

THE DRAGON AND THE DOVE
*A Bantam Book / June 1994*

If you would be interested in receiving protective vinyl covers for your
Loveswept books, please write to this address for information:

Loveswept
Bantam Books
P.O. Box 985
Hicksville, NY 11802

ISBN 0-553-44357-7

Published simultaneously in the United States and Canada

Bantam Books are published by Bantam Books, a division of Bantam Doubleday Dell Publishing Group, Inc. Its trademark, consisting of the words
"Bantam Books" and the portrayal of a rooster, is Registered in U.S. Patent
and Trademark Office and in other countries. Marca Registrada. Bantam
Books, 1540 Broadway, New York, New York 10036.

PRINTED IN THE UNITED STATES OF AMERICA

OPM     0 9 8 7 6 5 4 3 2 1

To Mark—who for my birthday
gave me Handel's *Messiah*, the Rosetta stone,
and a ruined castle in Wales.
Thank you.

# ONE

It was a shame, really, Jessica Langston thought, that anyone besides herself had their days held hostage by her eccentric employer. She cast another surreptitious glance over her desk at the Oriental woman waiting in the reception area of Daniels, Ltd. Two hours earlier the woman had given her a card identifying herself as Dr. Sharon Liu and had said she was there to see Cooper Daniels. When Jessica politely explained the futility of such an endeavor, the woman had only smiled and sat down to wait in the richly appointed office, sinking her elegant form into a wingback chair and balancing her slippers on the cinnabar-colored carpet.

Jessica could have told her again that she was wasting her time, but she had already implied as much twice since their initial conversation. Her employer did not see people without an appointment. For that matter, her employer did not see people with an appointment. Truly, she doubted if her employer saw people in any capacity. Jessica had worked for Cooper Daniels for two weeks and he had not seen her.

She hadn't seen him either—unless she counted the dusty oil painting stuck up on the wall in the darkest corner of the office.

Crotchety old man, she thought, giving the picture a bored glance. The artist certainly hadn't been paid to glamorize her employer. Cooper Daniels looked stern, unforgiving, wrinkled up, dried out, and like he could kick off at any moment.

Squelching a sigh of irritation, she went back to flipping through *The Wall Street Journal*. She hadn't gone for an MBA on top of an undergraduate degree in accounting and subjected herself to six weeks of intensive testing and interviewing by a gray-haired harridan of a headhunter named Mrs. Crabb to spend her days reading. She was supposed to be Cooper Daniels's assistant, not his receptionist.

She shouldn't complain, Jessica told herself. She was certainly getting paid as if she were assisting the owner and founder of Daniels, Ltd. in his Pacific Rim wheeling and dealing, as if she were tracking high-end real estate investment opportunities, which she'd been educated to do.

Dr. Liu rose from her chair and walked over to the large oak-framed windows overlooking Powell Street and the Bay, drawing Jessica's attention away from her newspaper. An olive-colored silk pantsuit with designer origins hugged the woman's slender figure; her hair was drawn back in a severe but regal chignon.

Jessica wondered how long she would wait before she finally gave up and left. The other woman's patience made her think Dr. Liu knew something she didn't, and that unnerved her. Any normal person would have taken her hints and left an hour ago. But that was the pot calling the kettle black. Any normal person wouldn't have spent the last two weeks working for a man whose very existence was becoming doubtful. Sometimes she wondered if he'd died and nobody had remembered to tell her.

"Ms. Langston, Cooper Daniels here. Please send Dr. Liu in."

The blue band of light blinking on her intercom and the accompanying masculine voice catapulted Jessica's pulse into overdrive and paralyzed her from the neck down. A barrage of questions spilled into her mind, adding to the general confusion: How had he gotten into his office without her seeing him? How long had he been in his office? What was she supposed to do?

*Respond*, came the answer. Regrouping quickly, she leaned forward and pressed the response panel on the intercom.

"Yes, Mr. Daniels. I'll send her right in." She turned to the woman standing at the window. "Dr. Liu? Mr. Daniels will see you now."

Jessica waited for Dr. Liu to retrieve her medical bag, then with as much grace as she could manage, considering her heart was pounding a mile a minute, she rose and stepped over to the ornate doors leading to Cooper Daniels's private office. Dragons with fangs bared and claws showing, wings spread and flames rolling, faced each other in frozen flight on the carved wooden panels. Surprisingly, the doors opened when she turned the handles. They never had before when she'd tried them, and she'd tried them many, many times—even going so far as to put her shoulder to the job and wiggle a bobby pin or two in the lock.

"Thank you." The Oriental woman slipped by her with a small smile that suggested, "I told you so."

Jessica responded with a tight little smile of her own, conceding defeat. The woman had known something she hadn't known. Dr. Liu had known Cooper Daniels was alive and well and in residence.

Before closing the doors, Jessica glanced into the office, intending to give the old man a nod of acknowledgment. He wasn't anywhere in sight. The only indication of his presence was the sound of running water coming from an open door off to the left, the sound of a lot of running water, as if someone was taking a shower.

After spending so many days looking at Cooper Daniels's portrait, she refused to dwell on the picture her last thought brought to mind, let alone take the time to imagine what Dr. Liu was doing there. Instead she made a quick study of the rest of the office, noting an ancient private elevator against the south wall—which answered one of her questions—the massive desk commandeering the north wall, and the elaborate arrangement of flowers and foilage cascading over a large, low table that anchored a circle of chairs.

She had turned to leave when a glimmer of gold caught her eye. She looked down and her next heartbeat caught for a second, captured by the dragon woven into the carpet. A hundred shades of bronze, yellow, copper, and brown edged the scales that began at the tail, where she stood with her feet perfectly placed in the heart-shaped point. Startled, she moved off the creature and looked up toward its head. Fierce emerald-green eyes warmed in the late-afternoon sunshine. Blue smoke curled out of the winged beast's nostrils. Flames of red and orange danced upon its tongue.

Fascinated and strangely wary, she let her gaze travel up the reptilian profile and down the crested rows of gilt scales. The animal was the essence of power, a force to be reckoned with, snaking across the cinnabar carpet and through a bank of white clouds in all its golden glory. And it was chained, collared at the neck by a broad iron band.

Dr. Liu discreetly cleared her throat, and Jessica's eyes flicked up. She knew she either had to leave or have a reason to stay. With the other woman moving about the large room with more familiarity than Jessica could claim, leaving was the only sensible option. When the shower was turned off in the adjoining room, leaving became the preferable option.

With one last intrigued look at the dragon, she closed the doors and walked back to her desk. She felt like she'd passed a horrendously complicated test of nerves and composure, something along the lines of "Can a person sit in a room by herself for two weeks and not have a heart attack when the intercom suddenly comes to life?"

Her smile returned in triumph. She'd passed with flying colors. Her "Yes, Mr. Daniels. I'll send her right in," had been delivered with unruffled efficiency, despite sweating palms and a still-jumping pulse. As soon as Dr. Sharon Liu left, she and Mr. Daniels were going to have to straighten a few things out. Outrageous salary or not, she wasn't going to spend her whole career waiting to say "Yes, Mr. Daniels" once a month.

An hour later her pulse had slowed to a near-comatose rate, she'd memorized a full quarter page of stock prices, and she'd decided she was leaving Daniels, Ltd. no matter what Cooper Daniels came up with as an explanation for his unorthodox behavior. She'd earned the right to be more than some old man's glorified secretary.

Besides, there wasn't any irreplaceable prestige in working for a company and a man no one had ever heard of, especially if the company was on the skids—which, given her work load and despite her salary, she was beginning to suspect. If Daniels was going to go bankrupt, he'd have to do it without her. She needed her outrageous paycheck, every penny of it.

Her MBA from Stanford University had not come cheap, emotionally or financially, but it had been the best chance she'd had of getting off the bottom rung of the corporate ladder. Stanford had been a chance to pull her life together after a dismal divorce, a chance to come home to San Francisco with her children.

Now she owed a bundle to Stanford and the government, and to her family for all their help. She couldn't afford to take a chance with Daniels, Ltd.

Before she left, though, she was going to ask her employer about the chained dragon. A man didn't have something like that splashed all over his carpet without its having some significance. What that significance might be, she couldn't begin to guess. But it meant something, something powerful. She knew it. She'd felt it.

"Ms. Langston? Cooper Daniels. I'd like to see you in my office." His surprisingly strong voice sounded on the intercom again without warning, startling her into another minor stroke.

Damn the man. She pressed a hand to her chest for a few seconds to calm her heart before pushing the response panel.

"Yes, Mr. Daniels," she said, silently swearing it would be the last time the words passed her lips. "I'll be right in."

She didn't know what to expect, but she knew what he expected. Mrs. Crabb had been very explicit about the high level of professionalism and creative intelligence required by Cooper Daniels, about the value of thinking on one's feet and being able to roll with the punches. Jessica had never doubted her supply of any of those attributes—until she stood outside the dragon-carved doors and prepared to meet the man who had kept her cooling her heels for ten-and-three-quarters working days.

The instant she stepped inside his office she realized she hadn't done nearly enough preparation. On the other hand, she consoled herself, nothing could have prepared her for the sight of a man who was young, healthy . . . and naked.

And that, she realized, was why most of her classmates at Stanford had opted for jobs with Fortune 500 companies or on Wall Street. At certain levels of success, people tended to take a bit more care with their appearance, most of them being dressed to impress—the operative word being "dressed."

Dr. Liu ignored her presence and continued working her hands down the warmly bronzed expanse of back bared to the California sunshine. The man was lying on a massage table that had been set up beneath the windows. His head was buried in his arms with nothing showing except an unruly mop of sun-streaked light brown hair. A discreetly placed sheet covered him from waist to thigh, but Jessica didn't have any doubts that he was naked underneath it—and she was mesmerized despite herself.

"There are two leather folders on my desk, Ms. Langston," the man said without lifting his head, confirming his identity as Cooper Daniels. His voice was unmistakably the one she'd just heard on her intercom. "The green one is mine. The red one is yours. Please familiarize yourself with the information in the red folder."

Jessica nodded in agreement, but made no move to comply, her gaze fixed on the sleek, powerful lines of his body. He was beautiful, like a sated animal in repose, oblivious to watching eyes and social decorum.

The curves of muscle in his arms flowed down from strong, broad shoulders to square, masculine hands. Dr. Liu moved to massage his legs, and Jessica's gaze followed as the other woman's long, slender fingers kneaded and soothed his well-muscled thighs.

Jessica swallowed softly, suddenly feeling overly warm. The Cooper Daniels in the painting was obviously a much older relative of the man in Dr. Sharon Liu's inestimable care.

"There is a stock offering on a company in Jakarta," her employer said. "They're trying to buy themselves into a major building project, a resort. I want you to find out the names of everyone involved in the project and then get me a rundown of their other financial investments."

She nodded again, embarrassingly dumbstruck, but able to rouse herself enough to step over to the desk. For reasons she couldn't explain, she became immediately aware that she was walking on the dragon. She made an unconscious move to keep from putting her foot into its fiery mouth. Another sidestep kept her from pressing into the iron-gray band around its neck. It was then that she noticed the words inscribed on the collar. Still heading toward the desk, she turned in a half circle to get the golden letters upright in her line of vision.

*By Love Alone*, she read, her eyebrows drawing together in disbelief as she came to a stop beside the desk. She read the words again to make sure she'd gotten them right. Then her gaze moved onward, to the golden chain attached to the collar. The gilt links wound their way through silver-lined clouds, until they broke free and found the dragon's master.

Her first thought was that not even love would enable such a delicate creature to hold the beast at the other end of the chain.

Behind her, Cooper Daniels groaned, a soft sound rumbling up from deep in his chest, and Jessica felt a disconcerting flush of heat sweep through her body. *By Love Alone.* She looked away from the white dove holding the chain in its beak and returned her gaze to the man stretched out on the table. He changed positions with languorous grace, drawing one knee up and turning his head to the other side with a deep sigh. Using a subtle move, Dr. Liu unfolded another length of the sheet before any really interesting part of him could be exposed. When he was covered, she continued to work her magic down his thighs to the backs of his knees.

"You have my most humble gratitude, *lao pengyou*," he said to the doctor. His voice had grown gravelly with pleasure, sparking another wave of heat through Jessica's midsection. The impropriety of him having a massage in her presence was nothing compared with the wild imaginings filling her mind.

He was the dragon—she had no doubts—but who was the dove? Not Dr. Liu, she knew. Despite the physical intimacy of the massage, Sharon Liu appeared to be professionally detached. She worked Cooper Daniels's body with skill and care, but not with love or tenderness. Not with the uncomfortable awareness Jessica felt while watching him.

She was out of line, way out of line, and for the life of her, she couldn't understand why he was having such a *sexual* effect on her. She had four brothers, an ex-husband, and a son. The male anatomy held no mysteries for her. The possibility of attraction was ludicrous. She'd been harboring a grudge against him for weeks, and she hadn't even seen his face.

He lifted his head then, and Jessica realized she was in deep trouble.

Cooper Daniels ran a hand back through his silky fine hair and narrowed his drowsy gaze on her. "Who are you?" he asked, the sultry pitch of pleasure in his voice replaced by a hint of confusion.

"Jessica Langston." She barely got the words out around the lump growing in her throat. She felt foolishly uninformed. Throughout her application and interviewing process, she'd never been led to expect anything like Cooper Daniels in the flesh.

The uncompromising angles and hard sensuality of his face emanated a wildness she'd never seen in any boardroom, a raw combination of threat and promise underscored by the greenest eyes she'd ever seen, eyes the color of emeralds, the color of the dragon's. His hair was longer than she'd thought, the straight fall of it brushed haphazardly off his face. He was unshaven, with beard stubble darkening his jaw.

"Try again." The words were delivered as a command, with all the confusion erased from his tone.

"Jessica Langston," she repeated, holding her ground and wondering if the line of questioning was another sign of his unorthodox behavior, or another test of her nerves. She didn't appreciate either, but knew now was not the time to call his bluff, not unless she was ready to lose. Her employer looked more than capable of eating her for lunch and needing seconds.

"I was very explicit about what I required in an assistant," he said coldly. "You are not it. Elise Crabb assured me Jessica Langston was."

She sensed his arrogance was as much a part of him as his breath, but he was in error. According to what Mrs. Crabb had told her, she met all of his requirements. If anything, she was overqualified for the job.

"If you will check my résumé and personnel file, Mr. Daniels, you will find I am more than capable of handling the job." She was also capable of her own arrogance, though she preferred to think of it as well-placed confidence. He wouldn't find many Stanford MBAs with four years of experience in the Far Eastern real estate division of a major insurance company. That her experience had been gained as a glorified secretary was irrelevant given her new degree.

"No, Ms. Langston," he said, acknowledging only her identity. "You are not capable of handling the job. What you are is a fatal error in judgment that Elise Crabb will find quite costly."

Jessica blanched, but managed to keep her gaze steady. A fatal error in judgment? She'd never been so insulted in her life.

She was the cream of the crop, the best. The only reason she'd accepted the Daniels, Ltd. offer was because of the salary and the location. A compelling combination, she admitted, but he was still lucky to have her, and if this was a test, she'd be damned if she failed, especially in front of an audience. Dr. Liu had stepped away from the table at the first sign of dissension and was looking out the window, but there was no way for her not to hear the argument in progress.

"You are dismissed," Cooper Daniels said after a tense silence.

"On what grounds, may I ask?" With effort, Jessica held her rising anger in check and maintained at least a veneer of professionalism. If this was a game to him, he'd gone too far. If it wasn't, she deserved a full explanation before she threw his job back in his face.

He once again took his time in answering. But this wait was accompanied by a slow, scorching perusal of her body, from the toes of her black pumps, up the length of her black suit, to the V-neck of her cream-colored silk blouse. His gaze deliberately lingered there until she blushed. She felt touched, indecently so, which she knew beyond doubt had been his intention.

"Innocence," he finally said, his impossibly green eyes meeting hers with all the force of a head-on collision.

The last of Jessica's composure crumbled under the impact.

"I beg your pardon?" she finally managed to say.

"Innocence," he repeated. "You've got it, and I don't want it."

"That's ridiculous," she said, surprised into candor.

"It's also the truth," he said without apology. "You are dismissed." He settled himself back down on the table, turning his head away from her and cradling it in his arms. Dr. Liu returned to his side and began massaging the soles of his feet.

The hell she was dismissed, Jessica thought. She'd never heard such drivel. Innocent? Her? She was the single mother of two children, who had been dumped by her husband when he had needed to "find himself," apparently in the arms of another woman.

"As your assistant, Mr. Daniels," she said firmly, refusing to concede anything at this point, "I have to counsel against such an unfounded, judgmental, highly subjective statement. It could cost you millions in court."

"Not if you want a reference," he said, then muttered a curse when Dr. Liu moved away again.

"I think you've underestimated my integrity."

"And I think you've underestimated my authority."

Since there was no reasonable way to counter his statement, she let it slide and chose an alternate approach.

"We have a legally binding contract, which promises a twenty-day grace period from any decision of termination unless agreed to by both parties." She'd been tossed out on her backside once, and the experience had taught her the necessity of working with a net. The special clause was her version of a parachute. It was far from golden, but it was there.

"You've had your twenty days," was his reply.

"The contract states twenty working days," she said without hesitation, sensing victory. So help her, she would have the satisfaction of quitting. "You owe me nine days, ten if you include the rest of today."

"I'll give you a hundred dollars for each of them."

She stiffened her shoulders and glared at the unseeing man who was treating her future and her integrity with such nonchalance. She couldn't be bought off, and certainly not for a measly thousand dollars.

"Five hundred," he said when she didn't answer. After another long silence, he swore softly and raised himself to his elbows. He cast a long-suffering look in her direction. "Ten thousand dollars, flat severance with excellent reference." An arrogant smile graced his mouth. "Take it, Ms. Langston. It is my final offer."

She had not graduated at the top of her class by being either passive or pliable—or innocent, for that matter.

"I want my ten days," she said, fully aware that she'd just had a cataclysmic change of mind. She would walk out in ten days, gladly, but she'd be damned if she let him throw her out.

Cooper respected tenacity and stubbornness. One or the other, and sometimes both, had been the only things between him and death at times. There was something to be said for being too damn stubborn to let go of a job . . . or to let go of life. He respected integrity, too, though by necessity it was usually one of the first things to go in his business, right after innocence.

He let his gaze travel the length of Jessica Langston

again. She was attractive, decidedly so, but not beautiful in a classically California way. Her curves were too rounded, her mouth too determined, her posture too severe, yet there was a dangerous softness about her. She was not what he'd been led to expect. She was not what he wanted.

He was going up against the she-devil of the South China Sea, a woman without shame or fear. He needed somebody by his side who could hold her own in bad company, somebody who didn't hesitate to win at any cost.

He'd asked for a female shark with a finely honed instinct for the jugular, and the most renowned headhunter on the West Coast had sent him an angelfish in silk. The pricey material draped Jessica Langston's breasts, caressing their fullness. Her thick auburn hair was cut short in front, but hugged the back of her neck almost to her shoulders. The softness he refused to be responsible for appeared not in the set of her mouth, but in its generous shape.

She looked kissable, a thought so untenable that it made him smile. Cooper needed an assistant. For reasons that had everything to do with mental acuity and nothing to do with physical attributes, he wanted a woman. He did not have to hire one with great legs, pale, pretty skin, and auburn hair. He would not hire one who even remotely made him think of sex, and when he looked at Jessica Langston, the thought was far from remote.

"Ten days," he agreed, meeting her cinnamon-colored eyes, his decision made. "You'll spend five of them in London. Take the green folder, leave the red. It's a long flight, Ms. Langston, and it leaves at six o'clock tomorrow morning. I suggest you go home and pack."

Jessica nodded slightly, hoping to hide her shock. Her mind raced ahead to the hundred and one details she would have needed to take care of before she could go out to dinner and a movie, let alone cross a continent and an ocean. She was a mother, for crying out loud. A fact he would know, if he'd taken the time to check her file.

Damn the man.

She turned on her heel and picked up the green folder. She had no idea what awaited her in London, and she wasn't about to ask Cooper Daniels. He'd never seen "think on your feet" the way she was going to deliver it. So help her, when she got back, he'd be begging her to stay—which would give her the ultimate satisfaction of saying no. She'd bet everything she owned that he didn't hear that word nearly often enough from the female of the species.

After she'd gone, Cooper reached over to the desk and picked up the phone. He punched in a call to London without bothering to check the time. George Leeds would talk to him no matter what time it was.

Jessica Langston wouldn't last ten days. She wouldn't last the five on her round-trip ticket to London. Cooper figured she would last exactly as long as it took her to study the green folder, deplane at Heathrow, take one look at George Leeds, and get back on a plane to the States with her resignation in hand. He was sure the finer points of negotiating bounty on maritime pirates with men like Leeds hadn't been covered in the curriculum at Stanford.

"Leeds," he said when a man answered the phone. After receiving confirmation, he continued. "I'm sending someone in my place. Her name is Jessica Langston. Any offer you wanted to take up with me, you can discuss with her, if she sticks around long enough to hear it. And, Leeds—" He paused until the man responded again. "Spread the word that she's under my protection. No interference will be tolerated. She's a business associate and I want her back looking as fresh and wide-eyed as she did when she walked out of here. When she leaves, I'll come and we'll finish."

He hung up and stretched again under the soothing magic of Sharon's hands. She was working on his left leg, his bad leg.

"You're healing nicely," she said.

"It hurts like hell."

"Would you like me to prescribe something?" she asked, her fingers gently probing the scar tissue that ran the length of his thigh.

In answer, Cooper gave a short, sardonic laugh. Sharon knew as well as he that there was nothing in her magical bag of herbs and acupuncture needles to stop his pain. There was only retaliation against the woman who'd had him maimed and left him to die. There was only revenge against the woman who had killed his brother.

He lowered his head and closed his eyes. He'd relived the scene a thousand times, and every time Jackson fell, Cooper found himself turning too slowly to protect his brother, or to protect himself from his brother's murderer. An explosion of gunfire sounded and a cutlass slashed him open from hip to knee before the dragon lady's henchman fell under his knife. All of it too damn late to save Jackson.

Jessica Langston didn't belong in his world. George Leeds was a peach compared with most of the people Cooper dealt with. He only hoped Leeds was enough of his usual self to offend her lovely sensibilities. Cooper didn't have time for a lawsuit, and he didn't have time for her, and he was surprised that he wished he did.

Damn surprised.

# TWO

In Jessica's book, jet-propelled takeoffs before dawn could only be rivaled by the first trimester of pregnancy for nausea potential. The added smell of congealed omelets should have had her stumbling toward the bathroom. Something more compelling, however, than both kept her glued to her first class seat—the surprising contents of the green folder.

She'd meant to look the folder over the previous night. She'd even cracked it open once or twice, in between wrestling with school schedules, transportation schedules, and baby-sitting schedules. The children's schedules and the children themselves, however, had kept demanding and winning her attention. She'd also assumed the green folder would hold information similar to the Jakarta stock offering in the red folder. If she'd had any idea of what Cooper Daniels expected of her, any inkling of what a low-down, conniving heel he really was, she would have made darn sure to take the time to study the contents of the green folder. She could have saved herself a plane trip.

As it was, the only thing that galled her more than what she'd been reading for the last fifteen minutes was the smirk that must be on Cooper Daniels's face as he lay in his warm bed, looking out at the fog-filled skies above the Bay, knowing he'd set her up.

The man was no world-class, upper-crust San Francisco nabob and financier. He was a bounty hunter, and he'd taken one of Stanford's finest and sent her to negotiate the price on a pirate's head, a Mr. Pablo Lopez from the Philippines, who had a penchant for ships of the Somerset Shipping Federation.

Jessica could hardly believe her situation or the nerve of the man who'd put her in it.

With a muttered curse, she flipped through the green folder again. Ship's manifests, oceanographical maps, sworn statements, and pages of handwritten notes all testified to large-scale acts of piracy on the high seas. Cooper Daniels was no run-of-the-mill bounty hunter. He went after men who stole the cargoes from hundred-thousand-ton oil tankers and eighty-thousand-ton container ships. The information explained a lot about the man himself. He didn't look like he belonged in a boardroom, because he didn't.

The question, though, was if she belonged on a plane bound for London and a man named George Leeds, the representative for the Somerset Shipping Federation. It was obvious that Cooper Daniels had hoped to get rid of her by putting her in over her head and letting her sink like lead weight.

He was mistaken in his assumptions, of course, as mistaken as she had been in hers. Given enough facts, she could negotiate the lease on a quarter section of an aircraft carrier's landing deck. Business ran on the laws of supply and demand. All she had to do was determine the tangible and intangible costs involved and set a fair price for the services offered.

That was all.

Damn him. She ought to get off the plane in Newark and take the first flight back to California. She should not let the problem intrigue her. She should not take up his challenge.

"Pirates," she muttered. Who would have thought pirates were still terrorizing ships on the ocean? Who would have thought there were men like Cooper Daniels out tracking them down and bringing them in?

She cast her eyes heavenward and blew out a sigh. Who would have thought there were men like Cooper Daniels, period? She certainly hadn't.

With an absent gesture, she turned one page, then another, stopping when she came to his handwritten notes. He had a strong style, bold and none too neat. He also had a very high opinion of his services, if the figures at the bottom of the page were any indication.

If she didn't want to be taken for a fool, she needed to do some research when she reached London. She could check the magazine and newspaper data bases on a couple of on-line computer services for anything that had been written about piracy in the last few years. Also, she could use her connections in the insurance industry to get actual figures on claims, losses, and premiums.

A small smirk curved her lips. She was perfect for the job, more perfect than Cooper Daniels realized or expected. By the time she returned from London, she would probably be able to teach him a few things about negotiating bounty. If she was going to London.

The decision to show him up couldn't be based on pride alone. She was too mature to let her ego rule her rationality. Well, almost too mature. There were other things to consider, like her wonderfully outrageous salary, her résumé, and that damned niggling issue of her self-esteem. She hated to admit it, even to herself, but she could more easily handle being dismissed as a business associate by Cooper Daniels than she could handle being dismissed as a woman.

It wasn't like her to want a man to notice her, but Cooper had noticed her. The way he'd looked at her, and where he'd looked at her, hadn't left room for doubts on that score. His heated gaze had sparked to life a purely feminine reaction, a reaction she thought had died with her divorce.

Logically, but against her better judgment, she had to admit to being intrigued by the man. Given the nature of their one and only meeting, with him being gloriously naked, stretched out like some sacrificial offering to Eros, it wasn't surprising that her mind tended to wander into forbidden territory when she thought of him.

The practical thing to do, of course, was to continue on to London and do the job she was being paid to do. Now that the initial shock had worn thin, if not entirely off; now that she'd looked things over and given the information some thought, she knew she *could* do the job, which left her little choice in the matter. That's what she told herself. Her ego, her pride, and her feminine responses had nothing to do with it.

She reached for her carry-on bag and unzipped the side pocket. After a quick search, she found a credit card and her address book. She used both to place a phone call to her old boss in New York. By the time she landed in Heathrow, she should be on her way to understanding the financial loss caused by modern-day pirates, the relative worth of maritime bounty hunters, and the needs of the shipping companies they both preyed on.

While she was waiting for her connection the flight attendant approached her with a tidily wrapped, congealed omelet in hand. Jessica blanched, but managed a wan smile before waving her on. Once the attendant had the offensive meal out of view, Jessica settled back into the comfort of her seat. Now that she knew what she needed to accomplish, the London trip should go smoothly, if not exactly pleasantly. There shouldn't be any more surprises.

Cooper stood outside the Boarshead Tavern, looking up at the signboard swinging in the wild English wind. Rain had soaked him near through, and he still had not found Jessica Langston and George Leeds. Ms. Langston had not taken one look at the green folder and his London associate and turned tail as she was supposed to have. Leeds had not taken one look at the woman and sent her packing. Rather, the two of them had hit it off and, according to Leeds's associate, Mr. Zhao, were even now carousing around the seedier dockside pubs of London.

The Boarshead was the worst of the lot. Cooper had saved it for last because it was the last place he would have expected to find his Ms. MBA-from-Stanford assistant. If she didn't belong in his San Francisco office, she most certainly did not belong in the Boarshead with the likes of George Leeds.

A fresh gust of wind blew up the river, snapping his coat around his legs, and Cooper pushed on into the familiar pub. He wasn't known for misjudging people. He found it particularly hard to believe he'd misjudged Ms. Langston. But her surprising affinity for pints and Leeds wasn't what had made him pay Concorde prices to get to England before the dawn of another day.

The Boarshead was dimly lit inside, with a few men leaning against the bar. The tavern's other patrons were scattered about a maze of booths and tables. Cooper's gaze skimmed over the seamen and bawds, looking for a woman who didn't fit in with the rest of the clientele. She should have stuck out like a sore thumb or, more accurately, like a hothouse hybrid in an untended garden. She didn't.

"Damn," he muttered. He was about to admit that sending her to London had been a bad idea when a woman's laughter captured his attention. He needed no other clue to locate the reason for his inopportune international flight. He turned toward the clear, fresh sound and began walking down the length of the pub to its farthest, darkest corner. He hadn't heard her laughter before, but he recognized it with the same certainty that he'd have recognized his own heartbeat. He wasn't pleased with the knowledge.

He'd waited two days for her to do her transatlantic flip-flop and show up with her resignation. The least he'd expected was the courtesy of an irate phone call. All he'd gotten was a fax Wednesday afternoon: *Negotiations with Mr. George Leeds, representing the Somerset Shipping Federation, will extend beyond the projected date. We are awaiting the arrival of Mr. Andrew Strachan from the North Star Line.*

George Leeds had his unsavory moments, but there were lines he never crossed when it came to women. Andrew Strachan had his noble traits, but none of them applied when it came to women, especially beautiful women.

Cooper had gotten on the plane because, as Jessica's employer, he had responsibilities for her well-being. She was out of her area of expertise when it came to dealing with Strachan. He'd also felt an uncomfortable measure of guilt for sending her off so ill prepared. Of course, that had been the whole idea behind his decision, for her to be ill prepared for a man like Leeds. That he'd thought about her more often than he'd liked over the last few days had been a minor consideration.

It had also been as compelling as hell.

She was sitting in the last booth with her back to the wall, and he wondered if the precaution was instinctive or learned. He knew Leeds wouldn't have allowed her to accidentally take his preferred spot. She had to have maneuvered herself into it, and for reasons all too obvious from Cooper's point of view, Leeds didn't seem to mind.

Light from an overhead glass globe cast soft shadows over her face and played with the highlights in her hair, giving her an air of mystery she had not had when he'd seen her standing in his office all wide-eyed and staring. Her iridescent blue dress was slightly disarrayed, baring one satiny shoulder. Unwillingly, Cooper followed the naked curve with his eyes. It was a sweet sight, but arousal and assistants were mutually exclusive by his rules.

Or they were supposed to be. Dammit.

He lifted his gaze to her face. She looked consummately at ease in the dreary surroundings, her smile flashing every few moments at what Leeds was saying, her hands embellishing her own words with graceful movements. She had pinned her hair up, and a few tendrils had fallen back down to curl against her neck. She was more than attractive, lounging in a buttoned and rolled Boarshead booth. She was beautiful.

She was also drunk. The lineup of empty pint glasses on the table didn't leave him a doubt. He'd never expected the woman to be so much trouble, or so damned tenacious—or so damned intriguing. Anyone else would have quit.

But not Ms. Langston, he thought with a grudging, wry grin. She looked ready to give everything right down to her virtue for the good of the company, and Cooper knew Leeds would be glad to take whatever was offered. Strachan, on the other hand, had never been known to wait for an offer. Fortunately, Cooper had arrived in time to save her from the Scots wolf.

He stepped closer to the booth, drawing her attention, and he knew he'd once again misjudged her. She wasn't drunk, not by a long shot. The look she gave him was lucid and piercing, with an element of surprise she quickly hid. As he took his final steps her gaze dropped to his bad leg and his limp. Her eyes softened, then she hid that emotion too.

"Leeds," he said, startling the other man into spilling his beer.

Leeds looked over his shoulder and immediately stumbled to his feet, his pockmarked face stark with surprise. "Coop, hell, man. I didn't—I mean, I didn't expect, or, uh, do anything. Nothing. I swear. Hell, look at her." He swung one brawny arm wide, encompassing half the bar before sweeping past Jessica Langston. The action upset his equilibrium and sent him tumbling back into the booth. Once his head got lower than his heart, the rest was history. Leeds slid under the table in a state of blissful unconsciousness.

Cooper didn't believe what he'd just seen any more than he believed what Leeds was wearing. The reprobate had on a suit coat with matching pants. He even was wearing a tie and, of all things, a collar bar, a gold one to match the ring in his ear. The man had gone all out to impress someone. When Cooper looked up, he found that someone scooting out of the booth, a concerned frown on her face.

"Now look what you've done," she said accusingly, pulling up the tight skirt of her dress so she could kneel beside Leeds's supine body. "You've completely unnerved the man."

"No, I didn't," Cooper said, his gaze riveted to her rising hemline. "I couldn't unnerve George Leeds on my best day."

"He was fine until you showed up." She tucked loose strands of George's gray-streaked hair into his ponytail and smoothed her fingers over his brow. "Dammit. He's out cold, and I was just this far away from closing the deal." She lifted her hand, her thumb and index finger barely half an inch apart.

"I thought you were waiting for Strachan." By his estimation, her legs went on forever.

"I came to the conclusion," she said tightly, "that it would be better for Daniels, Ltd. if I worked out the initial deal with Leeds. Then, if Strachan wanted to sweeten the pot, fine, and if he didn't, I would already have Somerset Shipping on board at our price. I did not expect you to show up from out of nowhere and frighten my client half to death."

She kept touching George, checking his pulse, loosening his tie, removing the ridiculous collar bar, and Cooper wished like hell that she would quit. He didn't like her fussing over the other man.

He felt his jaw tighten in irritation when she went so far as to unbutton the first two buttons of George's white shirt. Leeds had never worn a suit in his life. Never. His normal attire tended toward mix and match and cheap and serviceable, with a little leather thrown in for good measure. He usually had two or three earrings in his ear, not a single, discreet gold ring.

"What made you think Leeds would be more agreeable than Strachan?" he asked, as if the truth of the matter wasn't lying at her feet in a drunken stupor. Over the years he and Leeds had swilled enough gin and beer to float an oil tanker, and he'd never seen the old man flat on his back—until now.

"I checked Strachan out," she said, finally rising to her feet. "He doesn't have a reputation for taking women seriously." She smoothed her dress, and Cooper did his best not to follow the movements of her hands as she straightened her neckline. After her shoulder had been covered, he looked down just in time to catch the slight shimmy she gave her hips to shake her hemline back down to her knees.

"You checked him out?" he asked around the growing lump in his throat.

"I made some phone calls. Half of what I paid Stanford for was good connections. It's about a tenth of what you pay me for."

"What's the other nine tenths?" he asked. She'd finished rearranging her dress, which still didn't cure his staring problem. They were closer than they'd been in his office, and he couldn't help but notice things he'd missed then, like her scent, and the pale dusting of freckles on her chest and across the bridge of her nose. She looked sun-kissed, sweet, and sultry. It was a deadly combination.

He hadn't eaten much on the plane, and nothing since his arrival. He could only hope that was his problem. He did not want his problem to be her mouth and what looking at it made him want to do. That was trouble he didn't need.

He shouldn't have sent her to London. He should have sent her back to Elise Crabb and demanded a refund.

She met his eyes squarely and said, "One tenth is for my accounting degree, two tenths for my MBA, and two tenths for my natural intelligence."

"That's six." Damn, he thought. It *was* her mouth and not his empty stomach. He could tell by the effect watching her talk had on his groin.

She waited a moment before answering, and under her unwavering gaze, he felt sized up and measured from the inside out. He only hoped she wasn't able to read his mind.

"The other four tenths," she said, "are for not turning around and walking out when I realized that counseling you on your potential Pacific Rim investments wasn't going to take up nearly as much of my time as brokering your rather questionable skills."

"My skills are not questionable," he said, irritated with himself and her, and with all the reasons his body was coming up with for wanting to take her to bed. All he'd really wanted to do was fire her. He shouldn't have let his practical business side or his sense of responsibility get the better of him. He shouldn't have followed her to London.

"Your skills are not questionable in degree," she agreed, "but most definitely in form. I have serious doubts about working for a maritime bounty hunter, which I have surmised is the correct term for your line of business."

She was a cool one. He had to give her that much credit.

"You have six days left on your contract," he said. "I'll still give you a thousand dollars for each of them."

She ignored his offer. "I haven't figured out why you wanted an assistant of my caliber at all. An executive secretary could have met your needs for a lot less money. Right now I'm planning on counseling you to replace me with someone who can manage your office, and for you to do your own contract negotiating when the occasion arises, which Leeds explained isn't very often. You're usually on your own, bringing in the pirates for a price that was set without any input from you."

Cooper wasn't prepared to discuss any of her chosen conversational topics with her, especially in the Boarshead.

"Have you ever heard of anyone being too smart for their own good?" he asked, one eyebrow raised in warning, his implication hopefully clear.

She arched one eyebrow back at him, *her* implication crystal clear, and Cooper wondered where in the hell he'd gotten his first impression of innocence. The woman had the *cojones* of a rhinoceros, and she'd drunk George Leeds under the table.

Maybe Mrs. Crabb had been right. Maybe Jessica Langston was exactly what he needed.

God, he hoped not.

"Come on," he said, taking her arm. "Let's get you out of here before something happens we'll both regret."

Jessica would have balked on principle alone, but the strength of the hand on her elbow gave her no choice but to comply.

"What about Mr. Leeds?" she asked, looking over her shoulder at the man they'd left lying on the floor.

"I'll take care of Leeds after I've taken care of you," Cooper said.

"This really isn't necessary, you know," she said, struggling to keep up with him despite his limp. "I can take care of myself."

"So I've noticed," he said wryly.

She would have liked to argue with him, but their headlong retreat out of the Boarshead was having an unhappy effect on her equilibrium, and she didn't want to end up like George, especially in front of Cooper Daniels.

"Could we slow down, please?" she asked, inadvertently leaning into him. "The room is starting to spin a little to the left."

He came to a sudden halt and pinned her with a green glare. "You *are* drunk."

"No," she said, grabbing onto him for support. "No, I'm not. But I do have a limit when it comes to alcohol consumption, and I have reached it."

He swore, succinctly, looking right at her. That his words were spoken in a Chinese dialect did not confuse her in the least. She understood him perfectly.

"An apt sentiment, I'm sure," she said. "But I'd still appreciate it if you would slow down."

Cooper did, holding her close to his side to keep her from slipping to the floor, and holding on to his anger by the thinnest of threads. It was bad enough to have found her in the Boarshead with her companion inebriated to the point of unconsciousness. It was worse to realize what situation she would have found herself in if he hadn't shown up. He didn't have to look around to know how many men were staring at them. Half of them had probably been waiting for Leeds to pass out so they could move in on her.

Actually, he knew there was no probably about it, a fact quickly proved when a sailor still smelling of the sea stepped in front of them. The man was big and barrel-chested, with short-cropped hair. He wore a tight T-shirt that showed off a pair of sizable biceps.

"No need to call it a night, luv." He spoke directly to Jessica, ignoring Cooper. "Just because the old man weren't up to snuff don't mean you have to leave. Billy Ellen'll be glad to see you home, after we finish a couple more of the Boarshead's own."

"No, thank you," Jessica said with all politeness, giving Cooper a discreet push to direct him around the man. Cooper leveled a scowl at her. He didn't need her telling him what to do. Drunken sailors were his specialty.

"Forget the gimp, luv," the sailor said, moving in front of them again. "Stay and have a good time with Billy boy."

"Billy boy" was a wall of immovable chest and palpable aggression standing in Cooper's way and silently daring him to fight.

Cooper didn't need the added incentive of the dare. He was only too happy to oblige the oaf who had called him a gimp. In his present mood, he had neither the time nor the patience to suffer fools, so he flexed the muscles in his left hand and took a deep breath. The giant fell while he was still inhaling, before he'd had a chance to balance the tension in his muscles, let alone strike his blow.

The woman at his side brushed her hands together and straightened her neckline again. "I think you're right, Mr. Daniels. We should leave."

She'd tripped the bastard, put him to the floor, and she'd done it half-drunk. Cooper had seen it, but he hardly believed it.

Jessica slipped her arm through her employer's and ushered him toward the door before the man on the floor could clear the confusion out of his head. She'd had the advantage of surprise. She often did. She didn't look particularly athletic, she didn't look like a martial-arts disciple, and she certainly didn't look as dangerous as her employer. The sailor had made a wise choice in watching Cooper Daniels instead of her. It just happened to have been the wrong choice.

Once outside, she hailed a cab, and Cooper let her. The woman amazed him, and provoked him, and fascinated him. He remembered the look on her face when she'd seen him limping toward her across the pub, and he had an idea why she'd taken the initiative in dispatching the sailor. The thought that she might be pitying him, or that she believed he needed her protection, was damned aggravating and damned intriguing.

He needed somebody he could trust at his back. That somebody had always been Jackson, but Jackson was gone. The realization never came without an accompanying sense of loss, but it would never have occurred to him in a million years that the kind of protection and loyalty he'd received from his younger brother could be replaced, or that it could be replaced by a woman.

Jessica Langston had been hired to track the financial investments of Fang Baolian and to thereby bring down the dragon lady. He'd tried to fire her because he'd thought she wasn't up to the job. He'd thought she wasn't tough enough, or seasoned enough, or that the angelfish even knew where the jugular was on a man-eating shark.

He watched her flag down a taxi and lean inside to give directions. She knew what she was about. The last half hour had proven that much to him. A long conversation with Elise Crabb two days earlier had assured him that Jessica knew at least as much about the money game as she did about handling herself in the Boarshead.

That only left him with one problem—her legs, and her face, and her mouth, and the indefinable something that attracted him to all three. He had no business wanting her, but he did.

# THREE

Jessica sat stiffly in a high-backed chair, squinting against the early-morning light and watching Cooper Daniels prowl around the enormous sitting room of his suite. He was talking on the phone to George Leeds, his voice calm and low as they discussed the finer points of the deal she'd made for the capture of Pablo Lopez, the notorious Filipino pirate who was making a career out of stealing cargoes belonging to members of the Somerset Shipping Federation. Two weeks earlier Mr. Lopez had not bothered with unloading the cargo. He'd simply helped himself to the whole ship and put the *Callander*'s crew overboard. The Somerset people had decided to put a bounty on the brigand and to call in a bounty hunter. They had asked Leeds to contact the one bounty hunter they had all agreed could bring Mr. Lopez in alive— Cooper Daniels.

He was good. He was the best. One of the articles she'd printed off the data bases had mentioned an

American company run by two brothers that was building a reputation for hunting down pirates. The article was five years old and had been published in a European shipping-trade magazine. A more recent article in an American business publication had referred to a West Coast company working with London's International Maritime Bureau to clean up the coast off West Africa. Neither of the articles had mentioned Cooper or Daniels, Ltd. by name. They hadn't needed to. If she'd had any doubts about whom they were talking about—and she hadn't—George Leeds had made it clear why the bounty figures Cooper had scribbled in his notes were considered a fair price by the Somerset people.

Her employer walked toward the windows, and Jessica let him wander out of sight. Her pounding head wasn't up to dealing with the rare London sunshine streaming through the glass. When he walked back into her line of vision, he turned and faced her, and her cheeks suffused with color. She lowered her gaze, intent on smoothing nonexistent wrinkles out of her skirt.

She had been ready to show him up all right, she thought, to show him "think on your feet" and "roll with the punches." All she'd actually shown him was how well she could hold her liquor and how to execute a classic self-defense move. She was sure he hadn't been impressed. Businessmen did not pay Stanford prices for skills easily mastered by an eighteen-year-old with a sturdy constitution.

On the other hand, her last lingering perception of

Cooper Daniels as a businessman had vanished about five minutes after meeting George Leeds. She'd taken one look at the man's salt-and-pepper ponytail, the multitude of earrings in his ear, and had thought she was dealing with an aging hippy. Then, as they had shaken hands, she noticed the snake head tattooed on the back of his wrist. When she'd looked farther, she'd seen where the snake's tail came out of his collarless shirt and wrapped around his neck.

Despite her decision to handle these negotiations and figuratively wipe the smirk off Daniels's face, she would have turned and run on the spot, but George had had too strong a grip on her. Spread sheets and bond yields, stock prices and bottom lines were her milieu, not dragons and snakes. When he'd released her, she still would have run, if her hand hadn't immediately been taken up by another man. She'd been so overwhelmed by George Leeds, she hadn't noticed his companion. When she'd turned to the quiet, impeccably dressed Oriental man, much of her initial panic had dissipated. Mr. Zhao Ping, as he had been introduced, was more the type of person she had expected to be dealing with—professional, polite, well-spoken, and without earrings and tattoos.

"Ms. Langston," Cooper Daniels said, drawing her attention back to the present. He held the telephone receiver out to her. "George would like to speak with you . . . personally."

The inflection he gave the last word wasn't lost on her, and she wished George hadn't asked to talk with her. The two of them had gotten into enough trouble.

She stood to take the phone. "Good morning, Mr. Leeds," she said, maintaining a verbal distance and resisting the urge to turn her back on Cooper for added privacy.

"Good mornin', Jessie. He weren't too hard on you, was he? I never expected him to come after us in the Boarshead or we would've stayed someplace more respectable."

"I appreciate your concern," she said.

"Of course, if we'd only stayed in the respectable places, you wouldn't have seen what you wanted to see."

"Of course," she said, uncomfortably aware of her employer's nearness. She'd asked George to take her to the places Cooper usually went. It was professional curiosity, she'd told herself. The man was as inscrutable as they came, and she could do her job better if she understood him better, even if the job only lasted another six days. Her request, she'd assured herself, had nothing to do with green eyes, sex, or dragons. Mothers didn't think about such things. She was simply curious.

"I heard you decked a sailor in the Boarshead," George went on, a noticeable chuckle in his voice.

"Yes, well . . ." was all she could manage before George laughed out loud.

"You tell Coop he's got himself one dandy little helper."

"I'll be sure and do that, George," she said, her

voice drier than day-old toast. Going from "a fatal error in judgment" to "a dandy little helper" wasn't the sort of promotion she'd been aspiring for.

"Right, luv." George laughed again, proving he was well aware of her sarcasm. After a short pause, he turned the conversation to a more serious vein. "There were a few things I didn't get around to telling you last night. Things you ought to know."

"Such as?" she prompted when he hesitated again. She hoped he wasn't about to renege on the terms they'd hammered out over the last two days. The line she was treading between the law and criminality was already too damn thin to suit her. Despite her research, she wasn't sure under what circumstances extradition might become kidnapping, or if either applied to the deal she'd struck. She wasn't sure what the exact parameters were for the laws of bounty hunting, and the more information she got, the less sure she became. She did know that pirates were legally *hostis humani generis*— "enemies of all mankind"—and therefore under no nation's protection, which precluded the legal climate necessary for extradition.

That seemed to leave only kidnapping, and only because the Somerset Shipping Federation had decided against simply having Mr. Lopez killed, a small consolation Jessica was holding on to for dear life. She couldn't sanction murder. She could only do her damndest to prove to herself and Cooper Daniels that she was capable of handling any job anybody threw at her.

"Such as," George said, "you ought to go home

when you're done here. You're a sweet bird, Jessie. You don't want to get messed up with Cooper and his like. I know the business don't look too bad from London, and it probably looks real good from Coop's San Francisco office, but just about the time you get into the middle of the Malacca or forty leagues south of Singapore, a lot of bad things can happen."

Actually, Jessica thought the maritime bounty-hunting business was looking more appalling every day, even from the relatively safe environs of London. She had every intention of going home after this contract was signed. She had also had every intention of quitting Daniels, Ltd. when she got there, until those phone calls to her Stanford connections had given her reason to think otherwise. Besides checking up on Andrew Strachan, she'd discreetly checked out other employment opportunities. Her options weren't as varied as she'd hoped. California's economic slump was starting to reach even the upper echelons of the financial district, and Daniels was already paying her more than most of her colleagues were getting. Awful as it was, the pirate business was booming.

"Under normal circumstances, don't you see, I'd say you'd be fine," George went on. "But things ain't been atall normal with Cooper the last couple of months. It was a bad business, Jackson getting killed like that—out and out murdered, really—and I think it kind of put Coop about half a bubble off. He ain't been himself. I don't think he could take care of a ship's skillet right now, and I don't think he can take care of you, or that he'd even be inclined."

"I see," Jessica said, forcing her voice to a respectable blandness, working hard to hide her shock. *Murder!* George was right. The pirate business was no place for a sweet bird like her. Two days with the old man still hadn't inured her to the bombshells of information he was given to dropping. She turned sideways, giving her back to Cooper before giving in to her curiosity and whispering, "Who was Jackson?"

The action didn't do her any good. Even as she asked the question she felt the hairs rise on the nape of her neck. She was well aware of the cause. Knowing she couldn't very well hide herself or her conversation from the man staring a hole through her back, she casually turned around to face him.

The look he was giving her was anything but casual, and it should have prepared her for George's answer. It didn't.

"Jackson were Coop's younger brother," George said. "But Coop don't like to talk about him, so don't go mentioning me mentioning him, if you please."

Jessica blanched, her gaze instinctively dropping away from the anguish and anger reflected in Cooper Daniels's eyes. His brother had been killed, and he knew she'd just been told that. She wished she'd done anything except ask her last question.

Regret washed through her and left an awful feeling in the pit of her stomach. She didn't know where George thought Cooper might have gone that he wasn't listening to every word she was saying. She silently damned the man for not giving her a warning before she'd spoken Jackson's name.

"George, I—" She needed to get off the phone, but George didn't give her a chance. He kept talking, burying her in information, none of it what she would have expected to hear about the enigmatic man she'd seen warming his body in a pool of sunlight half a world away.

"It's a quid to a bloater that Coop will be dead before the New Year too. He's takin' chances, takin' on bigger people than he can chew, if you know what I mean."

She had an idea, a damn good idea. She swore under her breath. The conversation was quickly going from bad to worse.

She glanced at her employer, unable to stop herself, and found his anguish replaced by something less pained. In self-defense, she turned away, wishing George had told her these few things a damn sight earlier. If he had, she might have been long gone, instead of standing in a hotel suite, enduring the cold regard of a man whose reasons for disliking her were multiplying at an alarming rate. Enigmas never appreciated having their personal tragedies revealed to strangers.

"He was there when Jackson got it," George continued, dragging her in deeper. Despite the lines of courtesy she was crossing, despite Cooper's presence not ten feet from her, she didn't even hint that he should stop. She was already accused and condemned. She wanted the whole story. "I think seeing his brother cut down in the prime of life loosened a few screws. Coop's not playing smart like he used to. He's sold a couple of properties he shouldn't have at fire-sale prices when there weren't no fire. Not that I'm complaining, mind you."

Jessica understood the last piece of information perfectly. For all the impression he gave of being a bum, George Leeds was the consummate businessman who knew within a centimeter on any deal where profit turned to loss. He'd obviously been the fire-sale buyer.

"And I'm not complaining about the twenty thousand pounds he's borrowed either. It won't be me who cuts his throat if he don't pay up. But I'm not the only one he's into, Jessie. If I was to give you any advice besides leaving, it would be not to hold on to your paycheck too long."

Jessica swore silently again and closed her eyes, lifting her hand to rub her brow. She was beginning to get the picture George was laboring so hard to draw. She was working for a partially deranged, grief-stricken bounty hunter bent on revenge, who was willing to dismantle his whole company to accomplish a goal she did not even begin to comprehend, and her check was going to bounce.

"Who else and how much?" she asked.

The phone went dead before she got her answer. She opened her eyes to find Cooper standing next to her, his finger holding down the receiver button.

Her head barely reached his shoulder despite the heels she was wearing, but it wasn't his towering, overwhelming nearness so much as his stillness that unsettled her to her core. She'd never heard him move. She felt like a mouse who was surprised to find her tail trapped under the cat's paw.

Thick lashes shadowed his eyes as he took the phone out of her hand. The brief contact sent a slow wave of awareness up her arm, catching her off guard. Chagrined by her response, she admitted that his nearness had its disadvantages.

"Anything you want to know, ask me," he said coolly.

There were a million things she wanted to know about him and not one she dared ask about. Because in a completely different way, she already knew too much. She knew that the slope of his nose with its slight tilt on the end intrigued her more than it should, as did the texture of his skin and the smile creases in his cheeks—though she'd never seen him smile. She knew the smudges of weariness beneath his eyes concerned her, when they were really none of her concern.

He was close enough for her to see the pulse in his neck, to detect the tightness in the muscles of his jaw. He'd swept back his silky sun-streaked hair as he'd paced the suite, but a swath insisted on falling forward across his brow. Tension and energy radiated off him. He was alive and dangerously male, a predator's predator.

She knew enough about him to know she should stay away from him.

"Don't worry about the severance offer," she said, making her absolutely final decision before she could change her mind. There must be a hundred jobs in San Francisco that could meet her money requirements. She just needed to look for them. She took a step back. "My, uh, salary for the three weeks will be fine."

He placed the receiver in the cradle of the phone and lifted his gaze to hers. She was struck once again by the color of his eyes. They were mesmerizingly green, the hue of a shallow, sunlit sea. But traces of pain lingered in their depths, pulling on parts of her that had no place in a business arrangement.

"I think we're going to need more than three weeks," he said, watching her with an intensity she felt to the marrow of her bones.

She backed off another step, hoping she had heard him wrong. He couldn't possibly be asking her to stay on after she'd offered him an easy way out of their contract.

"We'll leave for the airport in an hour," he continued. "I'll fill you in on the details of your new project during the flight."

She stopped in her tracks, a sense of inevitable disaster coming over her. "What new project?"

"The one you were hired for."

"I thought you wanted to fire me." She was definitely getting in over her head this time. She could feel the water lapping at her chin. The job market might be tight, but Cooper Daniels's past was shady, his present no less so, and his future was bleak. She was smarter than to get involved with him.

"I did want to fire you," he said. "But last night you proved something to me I wouldn't have believed three days ago."

"What?" she asked incredulously. She couldn't imagine that holding her beer had impressed him enough to change his mind. He did not appear to be a man who changed his mind or his opinions easily, and he'd made his opinion of her quite clear.

"Underneath all your innocence, you've got courage, integrity, and tenacity. I need all three." He paused before adding in a quieter tone, "I need you."

She barely heard his last words, but they echoed more resoundingly than any of the others he'd spoken.

Every brain cell she had told her to turn around and walk away, and every instinct she possessed told her to stay and help. She knew how good she was. She knew she was an unqualified asset no matter how many leagues south of Singapore he got.

. . . *quid to a bloater Coop'll be dead too* . . . Maybe she was the edge he needed.

Maybe he was more than she could handle.

Damn.

She looked up at him and forced herself to hold his gaze. He met her challenge head-on, one eyebrow raised in a silent dare, allowing her to see whatever she might. They both endured the probing intimacy of her visual search, until heat raced across her cheeks and she had to look away.

George had been right, she thought. Cooper Daniels was a man on the edge, willing to risk everything. He hadn't hidden his pain or his desire; he not only needed her, he wanted her. The mixture was potent and devastating.

"I . . . uh, don't think so, Mr. Daniels," she stammered, turning to gather her briefcase off the hall table.

"You aren't dismissed, Ms. Langston," he said in a tone that stopped her in her tracks—for a nanosecond.

She picked up her briefcase in defiance.

"You owe me six days," he said behind her, and her hand stilled in its movement. "I want them."

Jessica knew she was caught. Her mouth tightened. Six days, she thought, mentally bracing herself. What could possibly happen in six days?

Nothing worth the cost of a lawyer, she decided. She would hang tough and wait it out. That left her with just one small problem to clear up with him.

She took her time, deliberately laying her briefcase back on the table before she faced him. She met his gaze straight on so there would be no misunderstanding. "No matter what you think, Mr. Daniels, I am not innocent, nor am I easily manipulated. It's my job to know the score, and I am very good at my job."

The smile she hadn't seen before came in a wry curve, deepening the lines on either side of his mouth and putting a teasing light in his eyes. His brows shifted subtly upward.

Jessica belatedly realized they weren't talking about the same kind of innocence. She also, on a deep instinctive level, realized that she'd been warned. She was playing with fire, the dragon's fire, and even more than she, he understood the allure . . . and the danger.

# FOUR

Cooper Daniels slept through the takeoff from Heathrow. Jessica had never seen anybody fall asleep before takeoff and stay asleep through the G-forces and engine whining. Not that he didn't look as if he needed sleep. She certainly needed sleep, but she hadn't succumbed. No, not her. She was wide-awake, breathing deep to keep her stomach calm and trying not to smell the tidily wrapped lunches stockpiled in the galley.

When the plane reached its cruising altitude, she was able to relax enough to pull some files out of her briefcase. There were a number of articles she'd printed out at the hotel that she hadn't had time to read. One of them estimated yearly losses to the shipping industry from piracy at a hundred million dollars; another guessed the losses were closer to two hundred and fifty million dollars a year. Her insurance connection had quoted a number closer to the hundred-million-dollar mark, but he'd also advised her that most acts of piracy weren't reported. Shipping lines did not want to get a reputation for not being secure.

George Leeds had also been a storehouse of information, especially about the seedier sides of piracy: the syndicates running out of Singapore and Hong Kong, the underground banking network able to transfer millions of dollars in a matter of hours, the kingpins with their harems of mistresses, the gambling, the drinking, the drugs.

Whatever Cooper Daniels's new project turned out to be, she was drawing the line at mistresses, gambling, drinking, and drugs. Money was her forte, not vice.

She shuffled the top article to the bottom of the pile and started in on the next, one printed in the *London Times*. She found little new information in the four-column spread until she reached the second-to-last paragraph. There was enough information there to make her sit up in her seat and take notice.

She carefully read the long paragraph twice before letting the article drop back on the pile in her lap. No one in the shipping industry liked to publicize piracy, so most thefts and hijackings were not reported by the news media. The *Times* article was no different in that respect, but to illustrate a point, it did summarize a story about a shipping line started in San Francisco in the 1880s that had gone bankrupt in the 1970s because of repeated pirate attacks. The line had been the Daniels American Line, more commonly known as the DanAm Line, and even more commonly known as the Damn Line.

The story made her realize two things: She'd been remiss in her original research into Daniels, Ltd. when she'd accepted it as the five-year-old international investment firm it purported to be. She also realized that even when sitting across a pub table from George Leeds, listening to all his wild stories, she'd underestimated her employer's ties to piracy.

"Damn Line," she murmured, skimming the article again and shaking her head.

"The old man loved that name," Cooper said around a yawn, his voice bringing her head around. "He thought it made him sound invincible."

He dragged his hands through his hair, and she watched the silky fall of it slip back into place, brown strands and blond finger-combed together.

"Ship with Daniels," he continued, grinning wryly. "Best Damn Line in the Pacific." He turned his head and leveled his gaze on her. "It wasn't, of course. Matson was the best damn line in the Pacific, and it galled the hell out of the old man."

"Your father?" she asked.

Cooper shrugged, relaxing back in his seat. "He preferred to be called Mr. Daniels, or sir. Mostly I just called him the bastard."

Jessica let the information sink in before she hazarded a guess about the painting in the San Francisco office. "You don't look much like him."

His grin returned, wryer and broader than before. "If I wasn't already overpaying you, that would get you a raise, Ms. Langston."

"You're not overpaying me by that much," she said in her own defense, then added, "If you didn't get along all that well with him, why do you keep his portrait in the office?"

"To keep his memory sharp and clear in my mind. It never pays to forget your enemies, Ms. Langston, not in my business."

"You considered your father an enemy?" she asked, not quite believing anyone's paternal relationship could be so bitter.

"Don't sound surprised, please," he said drolly, glancing over at her. "God, you are an innocent."

He had an infuriating way of delivering an insult.

"You make innocence sound like the kiss of death," she said, not bothering to hide her irritation.

To her surprise, he laughed. The sound wasn't sardonic, sarcastic, or wry, but a true laugh, a transforming sound that melted the weariness from his face and made her realize he was younger than she'd thought—younger and even more intriguing.

When he was finished chuckling, he looked at her again, his eyes alight with mischief. "Just so you know, Ms. Langston. A 'kiss of death' is something a sailor buys from a prostitute on the streets of Bangkok and it's about as far from innocent as you can get."

"Oh," she said, trying to maintain her dignity while her face turned a hundred shades of crimson.

"Not to change the subject—"

Thank God, she thought. He was going to change the subject.

"—but I'd like to spend some time familiarizing you with a lady named Fang Baolian."

"A friend of yours?" she asked, trying to keep the conversation going in the new direction. *A kiss of death*. She could just imagine what it was—barely. Maybe. She cast a glance at him, wondering if he'd ever had one. Then she chastised herself for prurient curiosity.

"No," he said, leaning forward to get his briefcase. "Not a friend. A pirate, the worst of the lot."

"Is she someone you're after . . . in a professional sense?" She ought to be ashamed of herself, and she was, but she was also curious. What kind of man was he, anyway? she wondered.

He snapped open the briefcase and removed a batch of files. "Until I get her," he said, "she's the only one I'm after."

"What about Pablo Lopez?"

"He's a stepping-stone to Baolian. He used to be her man in Manila before he decided to go out on his own. He should have stuck with Baolian. She never hits the same line or shipping federation twice in the same year, not anymore. By concentrating on Somerset, Lopez has made himself known and notorious. Somebody has to take him out."

The phrase, and the way he said it, set off all of Jessica's warning bells. Masking her alarm with a casual tone, she asked, "What exactly do you mean by 'take him out'?"

"Don't worry, Ms. Langston," he drawled. "I didn't hire you for the dirty work."

Somehow, she didn't take much comfort in his answer. She was tempted to ask him what he thought negotiating the price on a man's freedom was, if not dirty work. Instead she asked something else she'd been wondering about. "What did you hire me for?"

He spent some time organizing the files before he replied. "You mentioned a lot of the reasons yourself, last night."

"But not all the reasons?"

"The rest of it is a little hard to explain. I guess you could call it a last-ditch effort."

She hadn't thought she could slip any lower than a fatal error in judgment or a dandy little helper. She'd been wrong. Being hired as a "last-ditch effort" took the prize.

"A hundred men have died trying to bring Baolian to her knees," he continued. "I want her stopped. I think a woman can help me do it."

"A woman?" She didn't like the sound of that. She also wondered if his brother was one of the hundred men.

"Strictly behind the scenes," he assured her, looking uneasy for the first time since she'd met him. It was the only crack she'd seen in his armor of arrogance, and like his laughter, she found it remarkably appealing.

"I'm afraid I still don't understand," she said.

He was quiet for a moment, his unease obviously increasing. "Women . . . well, women are different from men. They see things where men see nothing, and they respond to what they see. I can't get at

Baolian by playing a man's game of strength. It's too obvious. She'll never let herself be outgunned."

"Smart woman," Jessica said while she wondered what it was he thought women saw that men didn't.

"She is that," he agreed. "But according to your transcripts and Elise Crabb, so are you—very, very intelligent. I'm gambling that if I give you enough information, you can tell me something about Baolian I never would have figured out on my own."

He was full of surprises. From what she'd seen of him so far, she wouldn't have taken him to be a closet feminist. Personally, she doubted if his theory about women knowing women would hold even an ounce of water, but she wasn't sure if she should tell him or not.

"I see," was all she said. She'd wait until she had a better understanding of what he wanted, if that was possible, considering the vagueness of his description.

"There's a million-dollar bounty on Baolian's head," he said, "partly because the people who are putting it up don't believe anyone will ever collect. I think they're wrong. People have weaknesses. Baolian's aren't manpower or firepower, or financial. But there has to be something she wants badly enough to come off her phantom ship to get. If I can get my hands on that, she'll have to come to me. The other possibility is that of all the pies she has her fingers in, one is more important than all the others. If I can find out which one, I can concentrate my resources on taking it away."

"Phantom ship?" she asked. Her questions about his resources, or the lack thereof, would come later.

"A stolen ship with false registration papers and a new paint job on the funnels. Every few months the papers and the name change, over and over, until they get caught fencing a cargo they acquired through fraud."

"Shippers don't check the registration's authenticity before they put their goods on board?" she asked, a little incredulously.

"Not enough of the time for phantom ships not to be profitable." He handed her an aerial photograph from out of the top file. "This is Baolian's ship. The photograph was taken four months ago, when the ship was known as the *Chin-lien*. It's as close as anyone has ever gotten."

Jessica looked at the small oval of what appeared to be a big ship floating on an expanse of gray water. "They didn't get very close."

He handed her another set of papers. "This is what I've been working on for the last two months, an inventory of all of Baolian's holdings, legal and illegal. Next to that is a list I've made of her business associates—"

"Legal and illegal," she interrupted.

"Yes. I want you to run down their holdings and cross-reference the two. I know at least two of the people she's done business with in the past are involved in the Jakarta resort. If that's going to be her crown jewel, then I need to get in. With enough leverage, I can push her out. Baolian doesn't like being pushed. She'll come after me before she risks losing face."

"And if her crown jewel turns out to be something else?"

"Then we'll go after whatever it is."

Jessica slowly nodded in agreement, more out of politeness than conviction. She was tempted to ask him if he'd ever heard of the proverbial needle in the haystack. She didn't, though. She was being well paid to go on his wild-goose chase, and she only had to keep the chase alive for a week. Then she'd be pounding the pavement, looking for another job with a more secure paycheck. Unless, of course, they could find a way to collect the cool million on Fang Baolian. A percentage bonus on that kind of take could smooth over many of her problems with Cooper Daniels.

The thought no sooner crossed her mind than she retracted it. Pirate hunting was not an appropriate career for a Stanford MBA, or for a single mother.

Or was it?

No. No, it wasn't. She was sure. Besides, working for a man she found devastatingly attractive was a package with doom written all over it.

Damn. She should have known the job was too good to be true. It was discouraging to hit a brick wall when she'd thought she'd made all the right moves.

"Mrs. Crabb never said anything about maritime bounty hunting," she said, trying not to sound too disappointed, or too bitchy. "Not in the whole six weeks she spent running me through the wringer, making sure I was good enough for you."

"The wringer, huh?"

She nodded. "She had a list of requirements as long as my arm and went on and on about how only the best was good enough for Mr. Daniels. She's either been misinformed about the nature of your work, or she's sweet on you."

He laughed again. "You wouldn't think she was sweet on me if you'd heard what she said when I called her and told her I wanted my money back."

"You asked for your money back?" Jessica turned on him, her pride plummeting another five notches. She couldn't believe it. He'd tried to return her like a bargain-basement sale item.

"I told Mrs. Crabb to hire me a man-eating shark," he said, a sinful smile curving his mouth and darkening his eyes. "She sent me you. I wasn't sure what to do with you . . . not professionally at least."

There was a compliment in there somewhere, but Jessica didn't think she dared to untangle it from the blatant insult.

"I also asked for brilliant and practical," he continued. "She told me you were both, in spades." A small laugh escaped him as he turned away and rested his head on the back of the seat. "I didn't ask for beautiful, but I'm learning to live with it."

Without any noticeable effort, he'd shocked her again. Another round of warmth crept into her cheeks.

"Mothers have to be practical," she said, becoming suddenly busy with shuffling papers around in her lap.

"I'm sure that comes in real handy."

She didn't need to look up at him to know he was grinning a mile wide, damnably cocksure of his ability to fluster her out of both her practicality and her brilliance.

Fourteen hours later they arrived in San Francisco, having left London at ten A.M. Friday morning and, by the miracle of time zones, reaching the West Coast at four P.M. of the same day. Jessica figured she only had five working days left to get through, and knowing she deserved at least one of them to sleep in order to recover from the trip, she revised her calculation down to four days.

Four days. Nothing of the magnitude he wanted could happen in four days. She was safe. And if on the off chance he talked her into the full five days, she would be okay. She was sure of it.

Stifling a yawn, she maneuvered through the other passengers crowding around the luggage carousel. She felt like a truck had hit her and not bothered to put on the brakes. Her back ached and her head was pounding from the hours spent in the air. She positioned herself to retrieve her suitcase, but before she could grab it, Cooper wrapped his hand around the handle and swung it to the floor.

"Let's go," he said, readjusting his grip and balancing the weight with his own suitcase and carry-on bag. "I've got my car here, so I'll take you home. It will give us a chance to continue our discussion."

Jessica groaned. They'd talked nothing but business since he'd handed her the files on Fang Baolian. She was all talked out. What he wanted to do was impossibly daunting. Despite the sizable amount of liquid assets he'd compiled over the last few weeks—selling off many Far Eastern properties he and his brother had acquired—she doubted he had the monetary clout to walk into any boardroom and force Fang Baolian out. She was sure what he wanted was crazy, but she wasn't going to tell him. No, she was going to keep the secret to herself. She was going to keep her mouth shut and her eyes fixed on the future—instead of on him, where they had a tendency to wander.

He fascinated her. He wasn't an easy man to look at, but she had surprisingly little trouble doing just that. In truth, during one of his naps on the flight, she'd memorized every angle and curve of his face, from the differing falls of his hair to the bare impression of a cleft in his chin. Most people didn't hold up too well under such close scrutiny. Cooper Daniels had done fine, much to her dismay. Admittedly, she wouldn't have had time to memorize anything if he'd been awake. Then he would have looked back, and the perceptiveness of his gaze was what made him hard to look at in the first place. That and the edgy emotion underlying his facade of calm. The laughter he'd shared at the beginning of their flight had become more remote with every minute spent discussing Fang Baolian.

"I have to make a phone call," she said when they came upon a bank of phones. "I'll only be a minute."

"Take your time," he said. "I'll be back."

She watched him walk away with a sense of relief. She didn't want to think about pirates anymore, especially one named Fang Baolian, and she needed a break from thinking about her soon-to-be ex-employer. The physical attraction she felt, had felt from the first moment she'd seen him, was embarrassing. It was probably perfectly normal, but even though she'd never felt another attraction as strongly or as suddenly, she was sure it was the type that made people do foolish things they later regretted.

To date, her ex-husband had failed to regret his plunge into adulterous lust, but she was sure Ian was the exception. She wasn't a prude, but she liked to think she had the maturity to make wise decisions.

Cooper Daniels was not a wise decision, and he wanted the impossible. He wanted her to follow a laundered money trail through an international labyrinth on a seek-and-destroy mission. He wanted to use his small financial empire to bring about the demise of a much larger one, even though his empire was crumbling. He wanted revenge.

Jessica wanted sleep. Not for the first time she wished she'd been thinking with more than her checkbook and her heart when she'd chosen Cooper Daniels's company over the ones from the East and the Midwest that had made her offers. She would never stoop so low as to go back to New York, the scene of her marital humiliation, but Chicago wouldn't have been so terrible. It wouldn't have been home, but it would have been bearable.

When a phone opened up, she stumbled forward, weary to the bone. She let her carry-on bag slip off her shoulder to the floor, then dug the necessary coins out of her purse and fed them into the telephone. Before anyone answered, Cooper was back at her side with a luggage cart. She gave him a quick glance and a halfhearted smile, a smile that turned genuine when a sweet voice spoke into her ear.

"Hello. Langston and Signorelli residence. Christina Langston speaking."

"Hi, sweetheart. I'm home."

Cooper saw the sudden beatific curve of Jessica's mouth, the soft glow in her eyes, and knew beyond doubt that neither of them was meant for him. They belonged to "sweetheart."

A pang of jealousy he hadn't expected tightened his chest. He had been without a woman's love for a long time, and Jessica Langston made him feel that lack with a surprising intensity. At another time, under diferent circumstances, he would have welcomed her into his life. He would have taken a chance with her, this woman who acted on his emotions and made him want to rediscover tenderness.

Hoping his jealousy was completely unfounded, he took a guess as to who her "sweetheart" might be— her nine-year-old daughter, Christina, or her seven-year-old son, Eric. He'd finally read her personnel file. He knew she had two children and was divorced from a private investigator in New York. He knew she was thirty-three years old. He did not know if she was seeing a man.

"Oh, Christina . . . yes, honey." She laughed, paused again, then murmured a reply into the phone. Cooper tried to remember the last time a woman had talked so sweetly to him. It had been a while. He could remember his mother talking in a similar way to Jackson—a green-eyed, dark-haired terror, the kind of wild child only a mother could love.

But that was a long time ago, and they were both gone now, his mother for more than half his lifetime and Jackson seemingly only yesterday.

Cooper felt the muscles in his jaw tighten. The pain never left him, the pain and the guilt. Jackson had been protecting Cooper's back when he'd died, and Cooper was supposed to have been protecting Jackson. He had failed, and that failure had left him devoid of any tenderness, any love. He had nothing to offer a woman. Nothing.

He swore silently to himself and gave Jessica an impatient look, motioning with his head. He was ready to leave. He'd been moving fast for the last two months, trying to outrun his feelings. Now was not the time to stop, not when he was bone-tired, and his emotions were seeping through mental and physical barriers thinned by exhaustion.

She said her good-byes and picked up her carry-on bag, which he transferred to the cart.

"Sorry," she apologized around another yawn. "But it's the deal I've got with them. I always call from the airport to give them a chance to whip the house into shape. Paul hates for me to think he can't handle the kids when I'm gone."

*Paul?* Cooper didn't remember anybody named Paul in her file.

"And Tony hates being taken by surprise," she continued. "He's always got something going on he'd rather I didn't know about."

*And Tony.* Cooper gave her a sharp glance. Even if she was seeing one man, she couldn't possibly be seeing two, living with two. The thought of one man was aggravating enough. He couldn't have misjudged—

He drew his thoughts to a sudden halt, realizing he had already misjudged just about everything else about her. He'd seen some pretty loose relationships in San Francisco, situations that would have easily accommodated a simple ménage à trois. One more mistaken opinion about Jessica Langston shouldn't surprise him.

It did, though. It surprised the hell out of him. He'd have bet money on her playing for keeps in the love department. Privately, he admitted that was part of her appeal to him. He liked to think there was someone left in the world a person could count on when things got tough. And things always got tough.

"I'd like to stop by the office for a minute," he said. "Will that be okay with you?" They had a job to do, he reminded himself. Nothing could get in the way of bringing Baolian down, least of all his hormonal response to the auburn-haired beauty who was his assistant.

"Sure," she said, sounding like she was past the point of caring about details.

"Fine."

More preoccupied with his new knowledge of her than he would have admitted to anyone, he led the way out to his car. Jessica Langston's living arrangements and her lovers weren't his business. Her employment was his business, and that should be uppermost in his mind. He needed her skills and her instincts, not her personal attention.

But he had liked having her personal attention all day. He'd liked sitting next to her, listening to her soft voice talking about his goals and questioning his assets. Her fragrance had eased him, her nearness had soothed him. Maybe he'd liked it all too much.

Jessica wasn't sure what she'd done to sidetrack him, but Cooper hardly spoke a word on their way to his car. His sudden quietness was a welcome respite from the information overload she'd been getting. Once they were under way, she stretched out in the warm and comfortable luxury sedan and let the subdued hum of the engine and the quietly playing classical music lull her into a state of relaxation.

"For the remainder of your stay at Daniels, Ltd., you'll be working under a strict operating procedure," he said from out of nowhere, startling her back into awareness.

She'd really thought they were done for the night. Sighing, she turned her head so she could see him.

"Operating procedure?" she repeated.

"Any requests for information will be done in the company's name. You've been sitting at the receptionist's desk for a couple of weeks. There's no reason for anybody to know you are anything except my receptionist."

She came more fully awake, her instincts telling her this was not an idle fancy of his.

"Why?" she asked.

"Precautionary measure."

For someone who had talked her ear off across most of the Atlantic and North America, he'd done an amazing regression into taciturnity.

"Precaution against what?"

He briefly met her gaze, his eyes assessing her with cool briskness. "Involvement," he finally said, returning his attention to the road. "Since you're not sticking around for very long, there's no reason for anyone to know you're involved. If everything turns out the way we want, great. You can put Daniels, Ltd. on your résumé and go straight to the top of another organization."

"And if things go bad?"

"Then you're well out of it." He ran his hand through his hair and shot her another glance. "You can tell people as much or as little as you like. I'll back you up."

He had a generous nature, she thought, which shouldn't have surprised her—considering the salary he was paying.

Given his show of support, she felt she should be more up-front with him. "I have to tell you, Mr.

Daniels, that I don't think too much is going to happen in one week." She tilted her head in his direction to gauge his reaction. There was none—except for a slight narrowing of his eyes. She pushed ahead. "The kind of investigation you want can take months. The kind of information I'll need can be very hard to track down. Then there's the time involved in determining the best course of action once we have the information."

She didn't consider her statements a concession of defeat before the game had even gotten started. She had more confidence in herself than that. But there were realities they both needed to take into consideration, and she hoped he was considering them.

"Call me Cooper," was all he said, checking the traffic before changing lanes to pass a car, giving a good impression of a man who hadn't heard a word she'd said.

Okay, she thought, drawing the word out in her mind. If he didn't want to take her seriously, that was fine with her. But now they'd both been warned. She just hoped he realized it.

# FIVE

Cooper took her up to the office in the private elevator. It was a throwback, he explained, to when the building had been owned by one of the old San Francisco shipping magnates who had gone head-to-head with the Damn Line and lost. Given the ancient workings and grumbling and groanings of the contraption, Jessica could only wonder in which century the battle had been waged.

The doors opened with a grinding noise, making each inch seem hard won. She waited, foot tiredly tapping, her chin down and her eyes lowered. When freedom was a few grinding seconds away, Cooper pulled her back from the door and stepped in front of her.

The rudeness of the action left her speechless. She hadn't burned her bras. She was entitled to a little consideration, and she wanted out of his ancient cage of an elevator.

"Excuse me," she said with soft sarcasm.

He had the audacity to flash her a grin over his shoulder. "We've got company."

She looked past him and realized he'd spoken with typical understatement. A number of Oriental men were crowded into his office, sitting around his table, standing against his walls, and walking all over his dragon. Most of them were dressed like businessmen in suits and ties, but one was not. He was dressed like a mandarin overlord, complete with arrogant demeanor and haughty composure. It took her less than a minute to realize the businessmen were actually the overlord's bodyguards.

"Remember, I'm paying you to think on your feet," Cooper said before stepping out of the elevator, his brief smile replaced by a more somber expression.

Those were the last words she understood for quite a while. Cooper greeted the silk-clad gentleman in a Chinese dialect and with great deference, an attitude she would have thought too alien to his nature for him to pull off convincingly. He proved otherwise with his low bow and his silent acceptance of the invasion of his domain.

During the introductions, she did manage to determine that the man's name was Chow Sheng. After a short bow that she performed without conscious intent, she settled into one of the chairs flanking the large, low table in the middle of Cooper's office.

She sat quietly, absorbing the nuances of the conversation if not its actual meaning, not quite believing she'd bowed to the imperious old goat.

With a clap of Chow Sheng's hands, tea was served

by two of the bodyguards. She could tell there was a discussion as to whether or not she should be included. At Cooper's indication that she should be served, a cup was offered with only a modicum of hesitation, just enough to put her in her place as a woman of little or no rank. She was appropriately offended, but didn't let her feelings show.

The amenities, if they could be called that, lasted twenty minutes by Jessica's watch, which she checked discreetly but often. Then, with no more warning than a shift of inflection in Chow Sheng's voice, the atmosphere became charged with tension.

Cooper stiffened beside her, and every bodyguard in the place responded with a not-so-subtle shift in his stance. All the awareness in the room was focused on the three people sitting around the table. The tension was palpable, hostile, and Jessica suddenly understood that she and Cooper were not at a tea party given by friends.

Under the table, she felt his foot nudge hers. She picked up her teacup and took a swallow, instinctively understanding she was not supposed to react to the new dynamics. She also understood the other implications of his action: He was aware of her; he was considering her presence and her safety. Or at least that's what she thought before he spoke, this time in English.

"I was not aware, Chow Sheng, of your new status as a lackey dog for the dragon whore."

Jessica choked despite her best efforts not to. They were fighting words if she'd ever heard them, and he was outnumbered. She quickly decided her wisest game plan would be to play dumb, defenseless, and inculpable, good guy to his bad guy.

"Fang Baolian's offer is most generous," Chow Sheng replied in perfect, unruffled English, pushing himself out of the deep comfort of the chair. "Five hundred thousand Hong Kong dollars to forget the unpleasantness between your house and hers."

"Tell her I'll see her in hell."

The Oriental man smiled blandly. "A certain rashness is required for your business, but of the two brothers, I always thought you were the more practical. Baolian's offer will be available for one week. Send someone if you change your mind." He walked around the table toward Jessica's end, his smile directed at Cooper as he said something else in Chinese.

Cooper responded in the same language.

Chow stopped next to Jessica's chair and spoke again, a soft questioning in his voice, his hand moving gracefully to her shoulder.

In an instant Cooper was on his feet with the old man's wrist manacled in his fist. Total mayhem would have broken out if Chow hadn't immediately raised his other hand to quiet the bodyguards.

Chow spoke again in Chinese. Cooper replied in the same language, his voice tight and threatening. When the older man acknowledged what had been said—by the barest gesture of his free hand—Cooper released him.

Studiously ignoring her presence, Chow clapped his hands twice, and he and his entourage exited through the reception area, leaving empty teacups and a surfeit of tension in their wake.

Jessica slowly rose to her feet and took a deep breath. She didn't know which was more disturbing: that Cooper had risen to her defense, or that she'd needed defending in the first place. From what, she wasn't sure, but she hadn't liked Chow Sheng touching her.

She should have listened to George, she thought, her heart continuing to pound too rapidly for comfort. Smart money would have her typing out her resignation before she left that night. It wasn't too late to jump ship. Now that she'd seen exactly what she'd gotten herself into, she should get out. Piece of cake.

She reached for her tea and took a hesitant sip, her hand shaking. It was obvious what she had to do . . . walk away. It was so simple.

"Damn," she whispered to herself, rattling the teacup against the saucer as she set it down. Nothing was simple. She wasn't walking away or jumping anything, and she knew it.

She had agreed to fulfill her contract, and she wasn't going to be frightened off by a little "big boy" pushing and shoving. With four brothers, she'd had years of hands-on training in dealing with macho posturing.

Of course, what had looked like an intimidating bluff on the part of the bodyguards had looked remarkably like a sincere promise of damage from Cooper Daniels. His willingness to protect her struck a responsive chord deep in her psyche, one she was sure she should have outgrown. It should have galled her to think she needed a man's protection.

But in a man's world, playing a man's game, having a man ready and able to protect her virtue didn't seem like a bad thing at all, even if it was macho posturing.

Not when the man was Cooper Daniels.

"What did Mr. Chow say that got us into so much trouble?" she asked when Cooper returned from locking the doors behind Chow and his gang. If she was in the game, and she was, then she needed to know all the facts.

He looked at her before walking behind his desk. At first she thought he wasn't going to answer her question, but then he spoke.

"The most honorable Mr. Chow," he said, seemingly disinterested as he checked his fax machine, "thought you looked too old to be a virgin, but noticed with great pleasure that your skin was beautiful, like white jade." He read the fax message, then turned and flipped a switch on his computer. The actions were automatic, casual, but the tension in the room didn't drop by so much as a degree.

"And?" Shocked as she was by the revelation, she knew there was more.

"He wondered if you would disrobe. If he dismissed his bodyguards, of course." His fingers moved over the keyboard, punching in commands.

"Disrobe?" Her voice was a hoarse croak of disbelief.

The typing stopped, and she could see the working of the finer muscles in his jaw. A perfectly silent moment passed before he shifted his gaze up to meet hers.

"I told him you would not disrobe under any circumstances."

She was grateful, but she sensed anything she might say would be inadequate, or worse, embarrassing.

"And that last bit of conversation?" she asked instead, even though she was afraid of what he might say. It seemed nothing was beyond Chow Sheng.

His eyes held hers across the length of the room, level and compellingly green, the irises still bright with the adrenaline rush caused by the confrontation. "When he accepted that you wouldn't disrobe in my office like a Chinese slave girl, he wanted to buy you for the night."

She'd been right. No atrocity was beyond Chow Sheng. His request was shocking and abhorrent. It was also curious and archaic. But curious begat curiosity, and much to her perplexity, she found herself asking the most awful of questions.

"How much?"

"Two thousand Hong Kong."

She did some quick figuring, and embarrassment blossomed full-blown. "Isn't that a little on the cheap side?" She should have had more pride than to ask, but a part of her hoped she'd made a mistake in her figuring.

A smile curved the corners of his mouth, and the brightness of adrenaline in his eyes was replaced by a glint of pure mischief.

"Skin like white jade can be a most desirable feature in a woman," he said. "But the lack of virginity is an irreparable flaw, which, under any circumstances, lowers the value of the goods in question."

As the goods in question, Jessica showed great face-saving restraint in her reply. "Of course."

"I probably could have haggled the price higher," he said, with only a hint of wryness in his tone.

"No," she said too hurriedly. "No, I think you did the right thing."

"Personally, I would have offered much, much more for a night with you."

"Thank you," she said, somewhat mollified. Then she realized her mistake. "I mean . . . uh, no, thank you. Not that I'm not . . . uh—" Oh, hell, she didn't know what she meant.

Riding home, she was still embarrassed, but she knew she had only herself to blame. Her last question had been foolish, unconsciously designed to humiliate herself—and it had absolutely changed her relationship with Cooper Daniels.

Once a man has turned down the equivalent of two hundred and fifty dollars for a woman and told her, it was damn hard to keep everything on a professional level.

What a day, she thought, and thank goodness they were finally heading home.

"Is this your exit coming up?" he asked, directing her attention to the freeway sign up ahead.

"Yes," she said, and spent the next quarter hour giving him directions through suburbia. Shortly before dark, they pulled up in front of a two-story house nearly overrun by a lush forest of trees interspersed with shrubbery, flowering plants, and ground cover.

And just about anything else a person could name, Cooper thought. There didn't seem to be a single species of flora missing from the mélange. A dry creek bed wound its way through gently sloping man-made hills, doing its best to anchor the profusion of green and growing things. A beautifully carved bridge straddled the creek on a brick path leading to the front door.

His first impression was of a jungle experiment that had gone haywire or been overdosed with fertilizer and California sunshine. As he looked longer, though, he began to see the hints of a design underlying the arrangement. The plants were also exceptionally well tended. Compared with most other yards, hers looked like a botanical health club.

"My brother is a landscape architect," she said, "working on what he likes to call a modified chaos theory. He's trying to find the bifurcation points of competing indigenous flora in an optimal but natural environment."

"I think they all won," Cooper said dryly, hazarding a guess about what she was talking about.

"That's what Paul is hoping will happen."

"Paul is your brother?" He turned to find her watching him, something she did a lot, though mostly when she thought he wouldn't notice.

"My next to youngest," she said, shifting her gaze back to the yard.

Her awareness of him lingered in the confines of the car, filling the space between them. He'd felt her gaze upon him many times during their long day of travel and even more so since the fiasco in his office. But then, as now, she was always careful to look away quickly. He hoped it wasn't because she saw too much. Her appeal to him wasn't something he could afford to explore, but it was strong, intriguing, and had damn near gotten him killed when he'd grabbed Chow Sheng. Rash didn't begin to cover what he'd done.

Reminding himself one more time to forget having a personal relationship with her, he shrugged off the recriminations for misplaced gallantry and opened the driver's door.

He knew they needed more than a week to accomplish his goal, even with Baolian already starting to cry uncle—the offer she'd sent via Chow proved that—and he was counting on Jessica staying on after her contract was fulfilled. He needed help, and he hadn't overstated her attributes. He was paying himself into bankruptcy to get those attributes.

He heard her door open as he pulled her suitcase and carryon out of the trunk, then he heard her sigh. The soft sound drew his gaze, despite his better judgment and his common sense.

She was balancing against the car door, lifting each foot in turn to remove her high heels. Her auburn hair had been finger-combed into disarray in the front, while the longer strands in back fell forward across her shoulders, skimming the delicate line of her jaw and emphasizing the fairness of her skin. Her blouse was partially untucked from her black skirt, making a white wing against the darker material. She was lovely, supple, and female, and her mere presence touched him.

Watching her, he was glad he'd stopped Chow from caressing her face, from feeling the skin he'd admired. She might be more stranger than friend, but Cooper felt a connection with her, one he was thankful he hadn't allowed to be sullied.

A part of him wanted to put her far away from the mess he was in. He'd requested a highly specialized accountant from Elise Crabb, a person versed in finance and the Far East, and she'd sent him someone he was thinking of more as a woman, as a mother, a human being. It was damned distracting. He'd wanted everything cut-and-dried, and all business. He didn't want any personal involvement. A robot who could think like a woman would have suited him fine.

"This is his house, Paul's," she said, looking over her shoulder at him and continuing her thoughts. "The kids and I share it with him and another of our brothers."

"Tony is your brother too?" he asked, wondering what idiocy had made him assume differently about her ménage à trois. Jealousy, probably, and that was hardly a comforting thought.

"The youngest," she said. "I have two more who are older than me."

He didn't know whether to be relieved or resigned.

His life would have been easier if she'd been seeing someone else, or two someone elses. He didn't want her to be available. His best bet was to get her suitcase to the door and make a quick escape.

"Hey, Jessie!" A deep voice called to her from somewhere in the jungle of the yard.

Cooper turned toward the sound, feeling a distinct but strangely displaced sense of recognition. When a young man broke through the foliage, Cooper froze. For an instant sunlight and shadow played tricks with the man's broad grin and the impish gleam in his dark eyes. For an instant Cooper thought he saw someone else.

"Jessie!" the young man hollered. He bounded down a hill to scoop her up into his arms and swing her around, making her squeal. A white daisy dangled precariously over one of his ears, held in place by straight dark hair that added to the painful illusion of familiarity.

"Tony Signorelli, you put me down." Jessica laughed and bopped her not-so-little brother on the shoulder with her shoe. "And what's this?" She reached for his flower. "Don't tell me you're playing—"

"*Jessie*," he warned, threatening to drop her.

"Tarzan and Jane." She squealed again as he let her fall a foot before he caught her.

Cooper was damned surprised at the playfulness of his Ms. MBA assistant, but it was the man who held his unwavering attention. Tony Signorelli was all energy and enthusiasm, and he was teasing his sister with a smile Cooper had last seen in the South China Sea.

It was Jackson's smile, an uncanny duplication of an expression Cooper had coaxed out of childish tantrums and endured through adolescent arrogance. He'd seen Jackson's smile quell dangerous men and seduce temperate women. Once, the woman had been Cooper's, or so he'd thought until Jackson had shown up and lured her away with his easy charm.

The reunion at the edge of the jungle was interrupted by the appearance of "Jane," a petite young woman with generous curves, short blond hair, and a warm smile. Her face had an elfin quality despite her plumpness.

"Hi," she said to Jessica, then lifted her hand in a wave to include Cooper where he stood by the car. "Hi."

Tony released Jessica and stepped aside to put his arm around the other woman in a gesture of obvious affection. His smile and his resemblance to Jackson faded into a more serious expression. "I'd like you to meet Alaina Fairchild. Alaina, this is my sister, Jessie."

"Nice to meet you," Alaina said. "Tony has told me a lot about you."

"Nice meeting you too," Jessica replied. With a lift of her hand, she also included Cooper. "This is my boss, Cooper Daniels. Mr. Daniels, my brother Tony Signorelli, and his friend Alaina Fairchild."

Cooper stepped forward and shook hands all around.

"Alaina is an accounting senior at Berkeley," Tony explained. "So I've told her a lot about you, Jess. Nice to meet you, Mr. Daniels."

Cooper nodded, silently agreeing that it was damn nice to meet everyone.

"Here, let me help you with those," Tony said, reaching for his sister's luggage. "We're all just sitting down to supper. You ought to stay, Mr. Daniels. I'm sous chef at Balay, and I cooked, so it's not like you have to eat that stuff Jessie comes up with, and Alaina made dessert."

Cooper opened his mouth to decline the invitation, even though he knew Balay was a good restaurant, but before the words could get out of his mouth, another scream filled the air.

"*Mom!*" A young girl, all legs and flying dark hair, launched herself at his assistant, along with a smaller but sturdier-looking bundle of boy. Cooper reached out a hand to steady Jessica and found himself accidentally tangled up in the melee of hugs. It unnerved the hell out of him.

"Jessie!" yet another voice hollered, and Cooper started feeling like he'd brought home the Holy Grail. The newcomer had to be Paul, of course. There wasn't anyone else left. At least he didn't think so.

"Lime cheesecake with raspberry sauce. It's one of her specialties," Tony was explaining to Jessica even as she hugged her other brother.

"Mr. Daniels," a small voice spoke to him from about waist height.

Cooper looked down to see an equally small hand

extended. He shook it. He didn't know what else to do.

"I'm Eric Langston."

"Hello, Eric."

"You're not my father."

"I know." Cooper felt like he'd just landed on an unexplored planet.

"I'm Christina," another voice addressed him.

Cooper turned and shook a slightly larger, but infinitely more delicate hand. "Cooper Daniels," he said. Christina Langston looked like her mother, all wide cinnamon-colored eyes and pale skin with a dusting of freckles across her cheeks.

He turned back to Jessica to say good-bye and to ask her to do a little work for him over the weekend, but he got waylaid by another introduction to yet another tall, dark-haired man, her brother Paul, who shook his hand, but then didn't quite let it go. The dinner invitation was repeated a bit more firmly. Paul said something about wanting to get to know his sister's boss better, especially since the boss was showing a tendency to whisk her off to faraway places.

Cooper got the impression he was being sized up and analyzed by a man about ten years his junior, and a gardener no less. He would have laughed, if laughter had been at all appropriate. The strength of the younger man's handshake told him it wasn't. Cooper Daniels was invited to dinner.

He could have declined. He wasn't a stranger to power plays, winning through intimidation, or outright rudeness, and he wasn't averse to using whatever method met his needs. But the Signorelli brothers were trying to be nice, and they were doing it out of concern for their sister. Cooper could do worse than to ease their worries about him. He knew he'd have to put on his best face and work at being sociable. It would be an imposition on his naturally antisocial— even surly—inclinations. But he could do it. Prove to them he was a good guy, and maybe they would influence their sister to stay on the job until the job was done.

Charm and affability. He hadn't used either in so long, he should have a ready supply.

# SIX

"He's not what I expected," Paul said, handing Jessica another double shot of espresso for her to mix with hot milk. Everyone else was lingering over Alaina's dessert on the back patio, leaving the two of them in the kitchen with a second round of coffee duty.

"Who?" she asked, though she knew perfectly well who he meant. She couldn't believe Cooper had allowed himself to be coerced into a dinner-with-interrogation by her brother. She knew for a fact that he had enough arrogance to have delivered a flat refusal without a shred of guilt. She wished he had. Instead, he'd turned on more charm than she'd thought he possessed.

All she'd wanted to do was have a snack, be with her children, and go to bed. Instead, Tony had pulled out all the stops. Coupled with Christina and Eric's loving and excitement, she'd gotten an unwelcome second wind. She probably wouldn't fall asleep until four in the morning.

"The guy on his second piece of cheesecake," her brother replied, giving her a wry look. "The guy who sent you overseas with less than a day's notice. The man who made you miss Christina's piano recital. The one I haven't been real impressed with so far."

"Oh. You mean the one who fired me five minutes after meeting me and is now practically blackmailing me into staying?" She grinned.

Paul grinned back at her. "Yeah. That one."

"He's not so bad, really."

"I know," her brother said. "That's why he's not what I expected. He's been pretty high-handed with you. I guess I thought he'd be a real stuffed shirt."

"He's had a hard time of it lately." She poured the last of the hot milk into the espresso cups, yawning. Maybe her second wind was winding down. She could only hope. Because of the guy on his second piece of cheesecake, she'd had a hard time of it lately too.

She had not had a private moment to tell her brother what she'd learned in London about her boss's financial situation and recent family history, but had decided the news could wait until morning. She didn't want to take a chance of Cooper hearing her talking about his murdered brother again. The awfulness of it still had her shaken.

"Nice guy or not," Paul said, "you don't need somebody else to take care of, a wounded dove."

"He's not a dove, he's a dragon," she said perfectly deadpan.

Her brother gave her a look of pure skepticism, and she rephrased her answer.

"Believe me, Paul. Cooper Daniels can take care of himself." *And me*, she silently added. George had been right to tell her to get out while the getting was good, but he'd been wrong about Cooper's inclinations to take care of her. Those were up and running in full working order.

"Maybe," her brother answered, still looking doubtful. "But he sure spends a lot of time looking at you as if he'd like you to take care of him, if you know what I mean."

"That's ridiculous," she said, turning aside as much to put the filled *latte* cups on a tray as to hide her sudden blush. "He's been nothing except rude and demanding. Hardly the actions of a man trying to impress a woman."

Paul shrugged. "I know a guy on the make when I see one, little sister, and your boss couldn't keep his eyes off you all through dinner."

"You're overprotective."

"I'm realistic."

"You're barely kicking thirty in the back, and I'm over the hill. Therefore I am not your little sister," she said, reminding him of her four-year age advantage.

He only grinned down at her from his seven-inch height advantage and said, "Oh, yeah?"


It was time for him to leave. It had been time for him to leave an hour ago, but Cooper still hadn't managed to extricate himself from the Langstons, the Signorellis, and Alaina Fairchild. At dusk, Paul had turned on the lights hidden in the trees and along the paths leading through the yard. The effect was exotic, reminding Cooper of the finer places he'd been to in Southeast Asia, places where the very air evoked mystery and sensuality.

His gaze drifted to Jessica. She wasn't what she was supposed to have been, and the disparities were going to be his undoing. She'd made a quick change of clothes before supper, doing away with her business suit in favor of a long blouse and leggings with a blue-and-white seashell pattern. She'd worked her hair up again, which was becoming his favorite style for her. It exposed the exquisite nape of her neck, a place he wanted very much to put his mouth to and taste with his tongue.

He felt a tightening in his groin and swore silently as he shifted in his chair. She was going to be the death of him. In four days of working for him, she hadn't made a false move—except for shaking his concentration and somehow making him care, making him want her.

He forced his attention back to his wineglass, lifting it to drain its contents. He knew better than to do what he was considering but he didn't think that was going to be enough to stop him.

"More wine, Mr. Daniels?" Tony asked.

Cooper looked over at the younger man and shook his head. "No, thank you."

Jessica's brother was a nice kid, nothing at all like Jackson, except in his smile, his exuberance, and his appreciation of the gentler sex. Alaina Fairchild was glowing under all his attention. Tony's basic body build and the darkness of his hair were the same as Jackson's, but without the smile to transform them, the resemblance was purely superficial. *Thank God.*

After dessert had been served, Paul had turned off the brighter patio lights, leaving Cooper with a sense of being cocooned in a rainforest night filled with stars. The lush landscaping extended along both sides of the house and overwhelmed the backyard with the same undiminished vigor it displayed in the front yard. The smells were wonderful, rich and earthy with a hint of flowers.

His own home smelled of the sea—and of emptiness. He knew that was another reason he'd allowed himself to linger. He hadn't hardly been home in two months, and he still wasn't ready to face the emptiness. Cooper had friends, but they were all mourning Jackson, and his guilt didn't allow him that luxury. It was safer to be with strangers, and he wanted to be with Jessica.

When Tony left to walk Alaina to her car, Paul gave Cooper an undisguised signal to leave. "I guess it's time we all called it an evening," the younger man said, rising to his feet. "It was nice to meet you, Mr. Daniels. Christina, Eric, this is it. Bedtime. Let's go."

The children stood up with their uncle, and Jessica followed suit.

"I'll see you out," she said to Cooper, then turned to her children and gave them both big hugs. "I'll be up in a minute, sweetie pies. We'll read a story together."

Rather than going through the house, she literally led him down the garden path. Cooper could have told her it wasn't necessary. He could have seen himself out. She was tired, and he'd already taken up too much of her time. But he wasn't ready to let her go. His quick escape had died with the invasion of her family, and he'd resigned himself to breaking a cardinal rule.

"I'll be going to Honolulu in the morning and staying over the weekend," he said, stepping aside and letting her precede him into a serpentine bower of latticework and grapevines. The arbor was lit from within by more of the tiny lights, but there weren't enough of them to do more than hint at the intricacy of their home. "I would appreciate you checking the office in the afternoons while I'm gone. I'm expecting some information on Fang Baolian. It will either come down by modem or over the fax, less likely as a telephone message. Regardless of how it's delivered, I don't want it lying around. You can store it, file it, download it, or transcribe it. I just want to make sure it isn't lost or seen by anyone else."

"Okay. I'll check in twice on both Saturday and Sunday," she said.

It was the kind of dedication he was paying for, and he would have been more surprised if she hadn't made the offer. Nevertheless, he was grateful.

"Thanks. I'll be back Sunday night. I'll leave my itinerary on your desk, in case you need to get in touch with me."

They walked a few more steps before she asked the question he'd been expecting.

"Do I need to worry about Chow Sheng?"

"No," he said without hesitation.

"You sound pretty positive," she said, not sounding at all positive herself.

"I am." Chow Sheng valued his life too much to trespass where Cooper had warned him not to go, and that was within a mile of Jessica Langston.

She looked up at him as if she expected more of an explanation, but she wasn't going to get it. Cooper saw no reason to repeat to her what he'd said to Chow. He was in a vengeful mood, he'd told the old man, a terribly vengeful mood. Only a fool would cross him in such a mood, a fool or a man intent on his own death.

"I didn't realize you spoke Chinese," she said, resigning herself to his answer with an ease he appreciated.

"I lived in Hong Kong with my mother for a few years, from when I was about seven until I was ten, and Jackson and I went back after she died. Her family is still in the trade and shipping industry there, Burnett and Company."

"I went to Hong Kong once on a business trip." She lifted her hand to brush back a hanging leaf. "The city is amazing. It must have been a very exciting place for you as a child."

"Not nearly as exciting as when the old man came to haul us back to the States," he said with a humorless laugh. "My mother became involved with another man, a Chinese. As much as my mother's family loved her, and as much as they hated my father, they couldn't tolerate adultery when it crossed color lines. They called the old man and told him to come get his estranged wife." He caught the shocked look Jessica gave him and knew he'd startled her with his revelation.

"How . . . uh, awful for you," she said. "I know adultery is very hard on—on families and children." She was floundering, and it took him a moment to figure out why. When he did, he wished he'd phrased his words less bluntly.

"I guess that sort of thing would be hard on kids as sweet as yours. But my mother only had me at the time, and sweetness wasn't my long suit. At one time I even liked the man."

"I wasn't talking about my children," she said in a flustered tone that made her impossible to believe.

"It's nothing to feel guilty or be embarrassed about, unless you were the one who strayed." He didn't expect her to reply to his veiled question, but neither did he need her reply. He'd done some checking on Ian Langston, enough to know what had caused Jessica's divorce.

When she didn't answer, he continued his story, partly to make up for embarrassing her, and partly, for reasons he didn't fully understand, because he wanted her to know what had happened.

"The fireworks really went off when good old Dad came and dragged her out of Hong Kong. Nobody thought she deserved the abuse he dished out, but once he got her back to San Francisco, nobody could stop him either. She died just before my sixteenth birthday. Physically, he didn't kill her, but he made her life a living hell. I always thought she just gave up when she couldn't take any more. I was angry with her for a long time for leaving Jackson and me like that, so angry, I packed us both up and took off for Hong Kong. Her sister took us in."

"I'm sorry, Cooper. I'm sorry you had to go through so much." Her voice was full of compassion for him, as if she truly felt and understood his childhood pain and wanted to wish it away.

She was years too late, but that didn't stop him from being uncomfortably aware of his emotional response to her sympathy. The urge to draw her into his arms and kiss her, to connect with her and offer her the comfort she was offering him, was almost overwhelming.

"It's always been even money on who raided the Damn Line to death, the Burnetts or my mother's Chinese lover," he said, hoping a few hard, cold facts would help him shake off the strange feeling he was having. He could admit to lust. Wanting to give and receive comfort was something else altogether, implying an emotion he hadn't suffered from in a long time.

He let his gaze drop to where the faint light rimmed the gentle contours of her face and haloed her hair with reddish highlights. He curled his hand into a fist to keep from touching her. *Soft, soft, soft.* Everything about her was so invitingly soft, making him want to hold her, to feel her in his arms. Her curves were soft, her skin, her voice, her mouth, her heart.

"You make me talk too much," he said, moving deeper into the arbor, leading her farther from the house. The smell of cedar and ripening grapes melded together in a rich fragrance, adding an intimacy he was all too aware of.

"Is Hawaii business or ... um, pleasure?" she asked, making an awkward change of subject.

By the slight wince he detected crossing her face, he could tell she wished she'd said something different. Her question had sounded more personal than professional, but that was fine with him. They were going to get a lot more personal before they reached his car, and he appreciated any help, however subtle, she gave him.

"Business. I'm picking up Pablo Lopez."

Her head came back up. "You know where he is?"

"Everybody knows where he is," he said, moving aside a trailing vine overhead. She stopped just on the other side of the vine, still well within the bower, her partially illuminated face reflecting her confusion.

"Then what was London all about?" she asked. "If everybody knows where he is, why didn't they pick him up themselves instead of wasting a lot of my time and contracting to pay you a small fortune?"

He looked down at her, taken back by the extent of her naïveté. He was a bounty hunter. She'd met George Leeds and been in the Boarshead. What did she think? That he spent a lot of time in boardrooms?

"They don't want to get hurt," he said, putting it to her as simply as possible. With a gesture of his hand, he suggested they continue walking.

She obliged him, hesitantly, for about three steps, then she stopped at the end of the bower. "And you do?" she asked. The concern in her voice was unmistakable.

"I don't get paid to get hurt," he said.

"But there's always a possibility." It wasn't a question, because he knew she knew the answer.

"I would like to get started early on Monday morning. If you could be in the office by—"

"Is that what happened to your leg?" she interrupted, showing the same tenacity he'd earlier thought was a virtue. "Did you get hurt trying to bring somebody in?"

"No. I was with Jackson."

He hadn't expected to tell her. He didn't know why he had. Everyone knew, but it wasn't something he'd admitted out loud, not in the nine long weeks since Jackson had died.

Damn her for getting to him, and damn her for making him want her so much.

Jessica felt the sudden change in him, felt the tension in him escalate, moving another degree closer to the edge. He was unpredictable, dangerous. He was off-limits. Any fool could see it, and she wasn't any fool.

Moonlight streamed down through the trees, silvering his hair and the chiseled planes of his face, highlighting the perpetual weariness in his eyes.

She shouldn't care, she told herself. The man was a self-proclaimed bastard.

But she did care.

He turned to face her, and their gazes locked.

"You do make me talk too much," he said, running his thumb along her cheek.

"I'm sorry." Her words were a bare murmur.

He moved closer, blocking the light. "I don't want your sympathy. I want your kiss." His hand slid to the back of her neck and his mouth lowered to hers.

He'd taken away the excuse of surprise. She'd known he was going to kiss her, and she didn't make a move to stop him. Worse, when his lips touched hers and parted, she instinctively complied with the silent suggestion that she do the same.

Without another preliminary advance, he slipped his tongue in her mouth, deep and sure, and she felt her knees weaken. He caught her with his arm around her back, drawing her closer and more intimately into his embrace.

No battle raged in her heart, no thought of retreat crossed her mind. If she'd had a minute, she might have been able to analyze her complete and unconditional surrender. She didn't have a minute. He tasted of wine and he brought pleasure, satiating, mind-numbing pleasure. It infused her senses and lit a flame of long-lost desire in her core. His mouth moved over hers and she clung to him, feeling only his strength and the gentle force of his intentions. When his hand glided down the length of her back and molded her to his body, she melted against him. When she felt his arousal, she melted even more.

Cooper felt the submission of her body, and everything in him tightened with ever greater need. The sweetness of her acquiescence swirled through him like wildfire, touching his chest, and his hands, and his groin . . . where her hips ground so gently against him. *Soft*. He'd known she'd be soft and giving.

He groaned into her mouth, unable to control the sound. He hadn't meant to take the kiss so far. He hadn't meant to let himself get to the point where his mouth was blatantly priming her for the act of love, where his tongue was stroking down the length of hers in a way that left no doubts about what he wanted to do with the rest of his body. He hadn't meant to get so hard so fast. He'd meant to taste, not to plunder.

But she had flowed against him with the first touch of his mouth on hers. She had responded, opened herself, and totally disarmed him of his planned restraint. A moment ago all he'd wanted was a kiss. Now he wanted to sink himself into her and slide deep. He wanted her softness to consume him, to soothe him and release him.

He'd lied, Jessica thought through a haze. It wasn't just a kiss. It was the destruction of her expectations. When he kissed, he meant sex, not "hello" or "good-bye," or "It's nice to see you." His kiss didn't say, "Honey, I'm home." It said, "I want to take you to bed. Now."

He desired her, and for a few sweet seconds she let herself revel in the knowledge. Then, of course, it was time to get back to reality—or so she told herself. She wasn't listening to herself, though. She was listening to him, to the rough sound of his breathing and the seductive noises made by the shifting of their clothing and the shifting of their bodies. She'd missed those things, the sounds of intimacy, since long before her divorce, and now this most inappropriate man was giving them back to her and setting her hormones on fire.

*I am a mother*, began the hallowed litany of reason, the prime directive, and Jessica latched onto it like a lifeline.

To no avail. As if sensing her attempt at withdrawal, he angled his mouth over hers to deepen the kiss. Her thoughts of motherhood fled before the sensual onslaught. He teased her with his mouth and body, moving in ways that were purely carnal in their intent and their effect.

She knew what all the sensations she was feeling meant, and she knew she had no business feeling them with Cooper Daniels, the fair dragon with the green eyes . . . and the body made of steel. It was a seduction in and of itself, the strength and power of him, the slow contraction of the muscles in his arms as he tightened his hold, the pressure of his groin rubbing against her in a rhythm guaranteed to make her lose her senses.

She moaned and tried to find a shred of inhibition to hold on to. When she did find one, she wished she hadn't. What was happening was suddenly so clear. Her own husband hadn't desired her, and she'd been the mother of his children. To a man like Cooper Daniels, she had to be an absolute charity case. He knew she'd been divorced for a long time, and tonight he'd found out she lived with her brothers. He'd decided to have a quick roll in the hay with the poor, man-deprived single mother, knowing he wouldn't have to work too hard for it. After that, he wouldn't want her hanging around.

Mortified by her conclusions, she broke off the kiss and pushed away from him. He wasn't quick enough to waylay her again. He did catch her hand, though, and when she tried to pull free, he made it clear he wasn't letting go.

"What's wrong?" he asked, his voice husky with frustration and need.

"Let go of my hand." She meant it despite the weakness of her delivery and the catch in her breath.

"No. If I let go of you, you're going to run, and I don't want you running away from me."

"I ought to bring you up on charges of sexual harassment." Her voice stiffened enough to sound at least serious, if not exactly threatening. But she was trembling, and she knew that robbed her words of even the slightest substance.

"Right," he drawled. "And I might do the same to you."

She blushed and was only grateful he couldn't see her in the dim light.

"Fine. I confess to kissing you." She was more than willing to accept guilt if that would help her cut her losses. She desperately needed to get away from him before she did something truly awful, like cry.

"That's not good enough, Jessie. I know you kissed me. What I want to know is why you stopped."

He'd called her Jessie. Only her friends and family called her Jessie, except for her ex-husband. Toward the end of their marriage, he'd never called her anything except Jessica, and disorganized, and boring. Cooper Daniels did not qualify as a friend, and he was as far from her family of upstanding citizens as a person could get without being arrested.

"I would rather not say," she said, putting as much professional distance in her voice as was possible under the circumstances. It was a pitifully inadequate amount.

"I'd appreciate a little consideration here." He tightened his hold on her. "I'm ready to make love with you, and thirty seconds ago you felt the same way. Now you don't. I want to know why. I know you're not a tease, and I know you don't scare easy."

He was being generous again; she felt like a tease. Her response to his kiss, to being held by him, shocked her. It had been a long time since she'd been kissed, but she knew that wasn't the reason he'd short-circuited her common sense. No matter what he must think, she wasn't that easy.

"Women have a lot of reasons for saying no. You're old enough to have figured that out." She hoped her answer would suffice and wished he would let her go so she could run away from him just as he'd predicted. If a person could die from embarrassment, she was in critical condition, and those damn tears were still waiting for a chance to complete her humiliation.

"I'm not interested in other women's reasons," he said, his voice softening as he released her hand. "I'm interested in you, and you can take that any way you want. Confession. Understatement. Indecent proposal."

She didn't look at him—she couldn't—but neither did she run. After a moment she heard him sigh, a heavy sound filled with resignation.

"Jessie." He tilted her chin up with his hand. His eyes met hers, steady and uncomfortably perceptive. "I'm as surprised as you are by what happened, but instead of standing here shaking, I'm standing here praying we can make it happen again. The next time we get this close, remember that. The next time we kiss, remember I want more, a whole lot more."

Jessica didn't think it was likely she would forget.

# SEVEN

The information Cooper had been expecting arrived at Daniels, Ltd. during Jessica's Sunday-morning office check. One look told her she wouldn't be able to store it, file it, download it, or transcribe it. What she could do was offer it a cup of green tea and a chair.

Everything about the "information" was foreign, from her short-cropped black hair, to the exotic tilt of her eyes, to her gray cotton pants and tunic, to the Chinese characters on the sheaf of documents she carried in a padded cloth folder. Everything about her was also very beautiful.

Her name was Cao Bo. Her eyes were a luminous amber-almond color and her skin a delicate golden hue. She spoke barely a word of English, but the few she had mastered were clear in their meaning. She had come for the Dragon, Cooper Daniels, for him alone, and she would not leave, or budge an inch, or say another word, until she had delivered her message.

After deciphering the woman's purpose and gauging the strength of her conviction, Jessica smiled politely and retreated to the sanctuary of Cooper's office. She wasn't up to another wait-and-see match with a beautiful Oriental woman, who undoubtably knew more about Cooper's whereabouts than Jessica did.

His itinerary showed his arrival time as eleven-thirty that night. If there had been a change, and he'd informed Ms. Cao and not herself . . . well, he was under no obligation to keep her informed of his every move. He'd only kissed her. That was all.

Jessica walked across the carpet to his desk, deliberately skirting the golden dragon writhing in flight over most of the floor. Her foot did squash down on the tip of the dragon's nose, but it was an accident.

He'd only kissed her. He'd only made it explicitly clear that he intended to do it again. He had said he wasn't interested in other women, that he was only interested in her, but men said the most self-serving things at times.

Of course, he had given her the key to his private office, which worked so much better than her bobby pins ever had. He'd also given her his on-line passwords, and while they'd been in the air over the Atlantic, he had spent an extensive amount of time explaining the use of international public-forum bulletin boards for exchanging information and holding cryptic computer conversations with his network of informants. Crime, he'd assured her, was as computerized as the next business.

She moved behind Cooper's desk and checked his fax machine. It was empty of a change in itinerary, as was the answering machine for the telephone. Her next step was to call his hotel; she was told he'd already checked out.

Jessica hung up the phone and tapped her fingers on the desk top. She wasn't at all sure she wanted him to kiss her again. She didn't think she had the strength for it. She also didn't think she had the strength to refuse him. Physically, he had a startling effect on her. When he'd been kissing her, she hadn't wanted it to end. His kiss had set off sensory fireworks, and he'd tasted good. So good, she'd spent too much of the last two nights wondering how the rest of him would taste, and wondering just how far she'd go to find out.

She knew she was heading for trouble, and now she had Ms. Cao Bo to worry about.

Unfortunately, neither of those problems was big enough to outweigh her worrying over Cooper. She simultaneously prayed for the week to end and dreaded the termination of her contract. She had nothing to offer a man like him, but she didn't completely trust herself to remember that. Her security lay in believing he was as certain as she that they were mismatched. He'd been way out of line with his kiss, and she'd been way out of line returning it with an eagerness that still astonished her. They needed to get a few things straight, and she wouldn't be able to do that if he got hurt.

If he came home injured, she'd worry and be angry, and she'd wonder how in the hell she'd gotten her hormones and her heart all tangled up with his. Being attracted to him was bad, but it was containable, controllable. Caring about him, though, would mean she was up to her ears in trouble.

At noon, Jessica sent out for two lunches to be delivered. She and Cao Bo ate in relative silence punctuated by smiles and small gestures of politeness—"Did Ms. Cao want more chips? Coleslaw? Tea?"

All offers were declined, and all told, Ms. Cao ate barely more than a nibble. Jessica's maternal instincts had been buzzing throughout the morning, noting the younger woman's unease that seemed a mixture of fear and nervousness, the almost unnatural brightness of her eyes, and her refusal to release her hold on the padded folder she held even while she played at eating. The lack of appetite was a final clue Jessica couldn't ignore.

"Are you sick?" she asked, leaning across the small table they shared in the reception area and lightly touching Ms. Cao's arm. Her hand immediately tightened. The young woman was burning up.

Jessica rephrased her question, putting even more concern in her voice. "How sick are you? Do you need a doctor?"

The woman shook her head in the negative, but her eyes told a different story.

"I think I should take you to the emergency room," Jessica said, realizing she'd let her other worries occupy her to the point of negligence. What she'd interpreted as nervousness was at least partially fever and physical discomfort, maybe even pain.

"No," the woman said, her voice tinged with desperation. "No hospitals, no doctors, please. I am only tired."

Jessica gave her an inquisitive look, her hand still gentle on the woman's arm. Either Cao Bo's pronunciation was improving with the increase in her temperature, or she spoke better English than she'd led Jessica to believe.

"To a hotel, then. You need bed rest and probably a couple of aspirin every four hours. And liquids. Lots of liquids."

"No hotel. I will wait here for the Dragon," Ms. Cao insisted.

"The Dragon—" Jessica caught herself and made the correction. "I mean, Mr. Daniels, might not be here until very late. You can't stay here for the rest of the day, not in your condition."

"I will wait."

"But I won't, and you can't stay here without me. That is against the Dragon's very strict rules." Jessica was making up the rules as she went, but that was what she got paid for—thinking on her feet. "I can take you over to a hotel very near here and leave a message for the Dragon. He can contact you when he arrives."

"No." Ms. Cao shook her head again, her eyes downcast. "No hotel. I have no papers."

Actually, she had lots of papers, right there in her folder, but Jessica understood what she meant, much to her chagrin.

"You don't need a passport to get a hotel room," she said, then wondered if she had just broken an immigration law by aiding and abetting an illegal alien. Cooper Daniels was going to be the death of her reputation, and she doubted if it would take him all week to accomplish the deed.

"No."

Jessica had to admit that Ms. Cao had that particular word down pat, with just the right amount of stubbornness to give it validity. "Okay," she said, continuing to think on her feet. Cooper wouldn't be too pleased if she let his "information" deteriorate into life-threatening illness, so she did the reasonable thing. "I'll take you home with me for a few hours, and when the Dragon arrives, he can come and get you."

When Cao Bo nodded in agreement, Jessica took the victory with a sigh of relief and went back into Cooper's office to leave a message.

As a matter of course, she checked the fax and Cooper's E-mail. Nothing had come in, but as she turned to leave, the phone rang. She'd had a few calls during the day, so it didn't seem unusual, until she answered it and heard the hoarsely spoken words. "Help. Coop . . ."

The line went dead before any more words could be spoken. Her first thought was that it was Cooper, and her heart plummeted.

Cooper found Jessica's message in his office a little after midnight, and within five minutes he was back in his car and heading for her house in the suburbs. He'd called first to tell her he was coming, but had deliberately kept the conversation short. She'd taken an operative into her home, and he was torn between blaming himself for the screw-up or blaming fate. He knew there wasn't anybody else.

The first thing Leeds had told him on the phone last Friday morning in London was to get rid of Jessie Langston. She didn't belong in his game, George had said. George had been right. There was no way for Cooper to warn her about every possible danger, not in the short time they had, and not considering the job they had to do in that short time.

The yard was dark when he arrived, but as he got out of his car the front porch lights came on, a beacon at the end of a long tunnel of night-darkened greenery.

She was waiting for him at the door, dressed in a T-shirt and jeans. Her hand was raised to her chest, her gaze searching him from head to toe, looking for the damage her note had said she feared had befallen him. He didn't miss the close scrutiny she gave his bad leg, as if she thought the weakest part of him would be the first to go.

Once on her porch, he stood closer to her than was necessary, looking down at her in silence, forcing her to meet his gaze. She looked up, flustered.

"Mr. Dani—" He lowered his mouth to cover hers before she could finish saying his name.

"Cooper," he said roughly when he lifted his head to look into her startled eyes. After the concern he'd read in her message, he figured they were solidly on a first-name basis. She drew in a small breath, her hands pressing against his chest, and he took the opportunity to kiss her again, warming her mouth with his until she opened for him.

The gentle, insistent stroking of his tongue along hers had an immediate effect on him and a desirable effect on her. The pressure of her palms lessened, and her hands slowly slid up over his collarbone, then his shoulders, and finally around his neck. She was softer and sweeter than he remembered. He wrapped his arms around her, holding her tight.

"I thought you were hurt, maybe captured," she murmured when he kissed her cheek. "I'm so ... relieved you're okay. It's been hell since lunch, and I want you to know you—"

Jessica pulled herself up short when she realized she was babbling. When the first tear spilled over, she got angry and pushed herself away from him. "Damn you."

"Yeah. I've had days like that too. But I didn't have enough balls to cry about them. Where's the woman?"

He could make a life out of shocking her, Jessica decided. "She's in Tony's room."

"Alone, I hope." He gave her a wry glance.

She ignored him. "She's ill, feverish. It could just be exhaustion. I wanted to call a doctor and have her looked at, but the idea upset her so badly, I decided against it."

"Good. She's justifiably paranoid if she's fresh off the boat. If she's been in Chinatown long enough to meet the kind of people who usually feed me information, she's got even more reason to remain as anonymous as possible."

Cooper followed Jessica up the stairs to her brother's room. He didn't tell her he wished like hell she hadn't brought the woman home. No matter where Cao Bo came from, someone was bound to have followed her, making sure she did her job, and that someone had been led to Jessica's house. It was all he could do to keep from hitting the wall with his fist.

They looked in on the young woman, keeping their voices low and their intrusion short. She was sleeping peacefully, and Jessica wouldn't allow him to wake her for questioning. A few more hours, she told him, wouldn't make any difference.

Cooper knew she was wrong, but he let her have her way, because he wanted to talk to her more than he wanted to talk to the mysterious Cao Bo.

"Can I use your phone?" he asked, following Jessica back downstairs to the living room. He had noticed the first time he was there that Paul Signorelli had a preference for animalistic furniture and accessories. One wooden table looked like a cheetah, a wrought-iron chair resembled a sleeping flamingo, and they both resided in a jungle of greenery that was not outdone by the landscaping of the yard. Cooper wouldn't have been surprised if it had started raining in the living room.

"The phone's in the kitchen," she said, and led the way.

"I know it's late, but would it be too much to ask for a cup of coffee?"

"No. Are you hungry?" she asked.

"Yes, but I don't expect you to cook."

"Tony's the cook," she informed him, walking over to the refrigerator. "And you're in luck. We've got an incredible pasta salad, cold crab, sourdough bread, and some indecent chocolate thing Alaina made for dessert."

"That would be great," he said. "But if it's too much trouble, I can have something brought over."

His wording was deliberate, and it didn't slip by her.

She looked over her shoulder at him, her hand on the refrigerator door. "You make it sound like you're not leaving for a while."

"I'm not."

"If it's the kiss, you misunderstood," she said calmly, but he noticed her grip tighten on the door.

"I wish it was the kiss, but it's not. You've got a woman upstairs who you shouldn't have brought home, and I can't leave until I know there aren't going to be any consequences."

"Consequences." She repeated the word dully, and he could see the full impact of the situation register on her face. She was frozen in place for a heartbeat before she half walked, half ran toward another part of the house.

When she returned a few minutes later, the panic was erased from her face, replaced by a steely determination.

"How are the kids?" he asked, guessing where she'd gone.

"Fine. Help yourself to dinner. I'll be back."

He watched her take a ring of keys from her purse and head for the basement. He could tell by the faint jingle and clanging noise coming up the stairs that she was opening a metal cabinet. Having a pretty good idea of what was probably in a locked metal cabinet in a basement—namely guns—he decided right then and there to call Elise Crabb in the morning and apologize for his doubts about the angelfish in silk.

After relocking the gun cabinet, Jessica came upstairs in time to catch the tail end of Cooper's telephone conversation.

". . . for tonight at least. Bring what you need and call your cousin Yuxi. I want two men here."

She set a handgun on the kitchen counter, within easy reach, and started to make a pot of coffee. The .357-caliber Magnum had been the ninth and last wedding anniversary present from her ex-husband. She'd thought it was an odd present, and had only realized later that it had been a big clue that he wasn't going to be around much from then on, especially at night. He'd replaced the security of his presence with the security of a gun so he could go his roving way with a clear conscience. She'd been furious with herself for being so blind back then, and she was furious with herself now, though for a different reason.

"I don't really think it's as bad as I made it sound," Cooper said behind her after he'd hung up the phone. "I just don't want to take any chances."

"I don't either," she said, tight-lipped. She finished pouring water into the coffee machine, and when it spilled, she swore softly and grabbed a towel to mop up. "Who did you call?"

"My houseboy, John Liu, Dr. Liu's brother."

"Your houseboy does double duty as a security guard?" She hated the tremor in her voice. Dammit, she wasn't naive. She knew the score when it came to the good guys and the bad guys. It was a game she'd grown up in, and one she'd married into.

"It's more like my security guard doing double duty as a houseboy."

She shook her head in disbelief. "Good Lord, Cooper. What kind of life do you lead?"

He was silent for a small eternity before he said, "Not an easy one since Jackson died."

The edge in his voice caused her to turn around and look at him, the damp towel still in her hand. He was rumpled, and tired, and gorgeous. She shouldn't care, she told herself. There was nothing in him except trouble and danger—and an anger born of pain.

"You can blame me for this problem," he said, running his hand through his hair, his eyes closing out of sheer weariness.

"I could," she agreed, setting the towel aside and wiping her hands on the front of her jeans. "But then I'd only be half-right."

His eyes opened, capturing her gaze. "If I'd been straight with you from the beginning, you would have made a different decision."

"Probably."

"There's no reason to blame yourself," he said, seeming determined to give her an out.

She didn't need him handing her absolution, and it was time she told him. "Yes, there is," she said, turning aside and punching the brew button. "If I had been thinking with my head instead of my ego, I would have walked out the first time you fired me. And for the record, I won't relinquish the responsibility for my decisions to anybody."

"I can respect that."

"You'd better."

They were at a Mexican standoff, and Cooper was too tired not to blink.

"I think I already know the answer," he said, "but just in case I'm wrong, do you know how to use that gun on the counter?"

"My dad was a cop for thirty years," she answered. "My ex-husband is a PI and I have two uncles and two brothers currently employed by the San Francisco Police Department, one as a martial-arts instructor. There isn't a Signorelli in a two-hundred-mile radius who doesn't know how to break down, clean, put back together, safely store, and fire that gun on the counter."

That's what Cooper had thought.

# EIGHT

Jessica woke with a start, her heart pounding, her senses alert in the darkness.

"Shh." The comforting sound was whispered close to her ear. "It's just John making tea in the kitchen."

John, Jessica repeated in her mind. John was Dr. Liu's brother, Cooper's security guard and houseboy. He was also a warrior. She had felt the power of his body in his handshake and in the finely focused energy of his dark gaze.

The voice whispering to her was equally easy to identify and recall. Cooper was a warrior too. He was also incredibly close, lying behind her on the couch, his body pressed against the length of hers. His hand moved on her waist, caressing her through the light cotton of her T-shirt. With effort, she resisted the impulse to lift into his touch.

"You haven't been asleep very long," he murmured, his breath warm and soft on the back of her neck. "Why don't you try to get more rest. Your brothers have gone to bed. John and Yuxi have everything under control."

Everything except you, she thought, and wondered how they had gotten into such a compromising position. She remembered meeting the other two men and settling on the couch to wait out the dawn. She didn't remember Cooper joining her.

He should have had more sense.

"Yuxi is checking the outside perimeters of the house and yard, and I just checked the children." His hand stroked over her hip and back down to her waist. The movement was gentle and caring, intimate and sensual.

She groaned to herself and covered her face with one hand. He wasn't the only one who needed more sense. She'd been divorced for three years, and her sex life had disappeared long before the divorce. She had missed sex, but she hadn't been compelled to search it out at any and all costs, not by any stretch of the imagination. She was a mother, a woman with responsibilities.

Now Cooper Daniels was touching her, his hand on her waist, his breath on her nape, his chest warm and solid against her back, and all she could remember was that she was a woman. It was nerve-racking, unsettling, and sinfully exciting.

His hand slid up the curve of her hip again, and she bit down on her lower lip to keep from making any sound. He had her trapped between his body and the back of the couch, surrounding her with his maleness and weaving a spell with his caress. She had to get up.

"Excuse me," she said so quietly she barely heard herself. Regardless of her abruptness, she hoped he would take the hint and move.

He didn't. His hand tightened and held her steady as he shifted his weight more fully against her. She caught her breath on a soft gasp, stunned by what she felt. He was aroused, the hard length of him pressed against her buttocks.

"You're so damn nice to hold," he said huskily.

"You—you can't do that here." Good Lord. They were in her brother's house, in the forest of the living room—yet despite the obvious constraints, she was on the receiving end of a quiet, inexorable seduction.

"I know," he whispered just before his mouth came down, warm, wet, and open on her neck.

Melting heat swept through her body. She groaned aloud, and his breathing grew ragged.

He gnawed on her delicate skin, running his tongue across her neck to soothe the love bites he gave. He was both rough in communicating his needs and gentle in eliciting her response, kissing her and shifting her in his arms until he could claim her mouth. When she was beneath him, he covered her completely, his size and weight controlling her with a tantalizing tenderness.

He felt like heaven, moving over her, using his body to tease and incite. His hand was under her T-shirt, cupping her breast and sending a wave of desire to pool in her loins. She'd forgotten how hot a man's hand could be. She'd forgotten how erotic it was to be wanted, how a man's needs could act as a catalyst to awaken long-lost passions. He rocked against her in the most primal of rhythms, and she wanted nothing more than to open herself to him, to welcome him into her core.

She grasped his shoulders, her fingers digging into his shirt, and he angled his mouth over hers for a deeper kiss.

It wasn't enough. It would never be enough as long as it was just a kiss. Cooper kept himself on the edge of no return, knowing there was no way on Earth he was going to get too much closer to what he wanted.

He wanted her. He wanted her with an ache he could feel right down through the center of his body, with the heaviest ache between his legs. He was hard . . . and she was so damn soft.

He broke off the kiss with a muttered curse.

His labored breathing filled the space between them, making him feel like a fool. He should have known she would go to his head like a fine wine cut with grain alcohol. He swore again, looking down into the most beautiful eyes he'd ever seen. They were languorous and confused, wanting what he wanted, but she had the same damn reasons for stopping that he had.

"Do I have a chance in hell of getting into your pants tonight?" He'd had to ask. He knew he'd put it crudely, but that was his only defense against the sure rejection.

She shook her head, and he could see tears forming in those beautiful, cinnamon-colored eyes. Women.

He wasn't angry with her. He was angry with himself.

"I don't suppose you'd like to get in mine for about five minutes?"

"And do what?" she asked, obviously shocked, her eyes widening with surprise.

The ingenuousness of her question brought a much-needed grin to his mouth. At least she wasn't going to cry now.

"You're a smart lady, Jessie. I bet if you give it a little thought, you'll come up with something."

She blushed, and his grin broadened.

His smile was short-lived, though, lasting no longer than it took him to feel her next breath bring them closer. He rolled off her before he forgot he had a few rules of his own when it came to women. He'd kissed her three times, and when he thought about it, he realized she'd either cried or been on the verge of tears all three times. That told him something he ought not forget.

He understood how sex might be considered physically threatening by a woman. He even understood how it could be emotionally threatening. In truth, he understood the emotional threat better than the physical threat, having experienced it himself. He did not understand why kissing would make a woman cry, and he wondered how many times he'd have to kiss her before he found out.

"Would you like some tea?" he asked, keeping his distance by walking to the other side of the cheetah table.

"No," she said, and he could hear her straightening her clothes as she stood up. "I think I'll go sleep in Christina's room."

He turned and watched her as she left, her silhouette making a shadow in the doorway in the instant before she was gone. It was a sensible plan, he thought. She'd be safe in there, safe from him.


They both looked like hell, like two people who hadn't gotten much sleep, and there wasn't a person milling around the kitchen who didn't have something to say about one or the other of them.

"You kinda look like a raccoon, Mom," Eric said, with that dark sitting under your eyeballs." He tilted his head back and gave her a scrunched-up scrutinizing. "It's neat."

"Thank you, honey. Eat your granola." Jessica sighed and continued rummaging through her purse, looking for the extra-strength aspirin she kept there. Children were so beautifully, simply, painfully honest. A mother's self-esteem didn't stand a chance.

Shoving aside her key ring with a small flashlight attachment and the paperback she always kept handy in case she got caught in traffic, she finally found the plastic bottle she was looking for.

"The woman is out back on the patio, Cooper," John Liu said, referring to Cao Bo. "She seems recovered from her ordeal. If you think you're up to it, we could talk to her now." A mischievous wryness shaded his voice. Cooper gave him a drop-dead dragon glare.

Jessica didn't bother to hide a tired grin at his expense. His irritability was the only solace available for her wounded ego. They'd gone further than a kiss in the night, and she was trying to figure out why. She was a mother, and mothers didn't neck on couches.

He and John refilled their coffee cups on their way out the door, with Cooper taking an extra cup for the messenger.

Jessica got up from the table and warmed her own cup, watching the two men walk across the first patio and drop down a couple of steps to the second level. Ms. Cao awaited them there under the shade of a tan-oak tree. Cooper really did look like hell. His hair was sticking up from all the times he'd plowed his fingers through it. Beard stubble darkened his jaw, and his clothes were wrinkled.

"Looks like he had a rough night," Tony said conversationally, coming up behind her and pouring himself a cup of coffee.

Jessica made a noncommittal reply.

"Hmm." Tony took his first sip, then said, "You don't look so good yourself."

"Thank you."

"I guess you should know Paul set him straight this morning," her brother said, reaching over her head for a cereal bowl.

She shot him a wary glance. "What do you mean?"

"Don't worry. He did it nicely."

"Did what?" She hardly dared to ask.

# Get Swept Away To Your Romantic Holiday!

**I**magine being wrapped in the embrace of your lover's arms, watching glorious Hawaiian rainbows born only for you. Imagine strolling through the gothic haunts of romantic London. Imagine being drenched in the sun-soaked beauty of the Caribbean. If you crave such journeys then enter now to...

## WIN YOUR ROMANTIC RENDEZVOUS PLUS $5,000 CASH!
### *Or Take $25,000 CASH!*

Seize the moment and enter to win one of these exotic 14-day rendezvous for two, plus $5,000.00 CASH! To enter affix the destination ticket of your choice to the Official Entry Form and drop it in the mail. It costs you absolutely nothing to enter—not even postage! So take a chance on romance and enter today!

## Has More In Store For You With
## 4 FREE BOOKS and a FREE GIFT!

We've got four FREE Loveswept Romances and a FREE Lighted Makeup Case ready to send you!

Place the FREE GIFTS ticket on your Entry Form, and your first shipment of Loveswept Romances is yours absolutely FREE—*and that means no shipping and handling.*

Plus, about once a month, you'll get four *new* books hot off the presses, *before they're in the bookstores.* You'll always have 15 days to decide whether to keep any shipment, for our low regular price, currently just $11.95.* **You are never obligated to keep any shipment**, and you may cancel at any time by writing "cancel" across our invoice and returning the shipment to us, at our expense. There's **no risk** and **no obligation** to buy, *ever.*

It's a pretty seductive offer, we've made even more attractive with the **Lighted Makeup Case—yours absolutely FREE!** It has an elegant tortoiseshell finish, an assortment of brushes for eye shadow, blush and lip color. And with the lighted makeup mirror *you* can make sure he'll always see the passion in your eyes!

**BOTH GIFTS ARE ABSOLUTELY FREE AND ARE YOURS TO KEEP FOREVER** no matter what you decide about future shipments! So come on! You risk nothing at all—and you stand to gain a world of sizzling romance, exciting prizes...and FREE GIFTS!

*(plus shipping & handling, and sales tax in NY and Canada)

# ENTER NOW TO WIN A ROMANTIC RENDEZVOUS FOR TWO

## Plus $5,000 CASH!

*or take $25,000 Cash!*

**No risk and no obligation to buy, anything, *ever!***

## *Winners Classic*

### SWEEPSTAKES
### OFFICIAL ENTRY FORM

☐ **YES!** Enter me in the sweepstakes! I've affixed the destination ticket for the Romantic Rendezvous of my choice to this Entry Form. I've also affixed the FREE GIFTS ticket. So please, send me my 4 FREE BOOKS and FREE Lighted Makeup Case.

| Affix Destination Ticket of Your Choice Here | TICKET | Affix FREE GIFTS Ticket Here | 🎁 |
|---|---|---|---|

**PLEASE PRINT CLEARLY**                CK123      12237

NAME

ADDRESS

CITY                                          APT. #

STATE                                         ZIP

*DETACH CAREFULLY AND MAIL TODAY*

There is no purchase necessary to enter the sweepstakes. To enter without taking advantage of the risk-free offer, return the entry form with only the romantic rendezvous ticket affixed. To be eligible, sweepstakes entries must be received by the deadline found in the accompanying rules at the back of the book. There is no obligation to buy when you send for your free books and free lighted makeup case. You may preview each new shipment for 15 days free. If you decide against it, simply return the shipment within 15 days and owe nothing. If you keep them, pay our low regular price, currently just $2.99 each book —a savings of $.50 per book off the cover price (plus shipping & handling, and sales tax in NY and Canada.)

Prices subject to change. Orders subject to approval. See complete sweepstakes rules at the back of the book.

**Don't miss your chance to win a romantic rendezvous for two and get 4 FREE BOOKS and a FREE Lighted Makeup Case!**

**You risk nothing—so enter now!**

"Told him about Ian."

Great, Jessica thought, not bothering to sputter out her indignation. Now her humiliation was perfectly complete. Someday Paul would grow up and realize that being the oldest man living in the house did not make him the oldest, most responsible person living in the house. He was her little brother, not her father. Macho posturing had its unbearable moments, and this was one of them.

"I don't know why he bothered," Tony continued, rustling around in the cupboard for his favorite cereal. "Looks to me like you and Cooper have it all figured out."

Jessica had no idea what he meant, and even though she was dying to ask for an explanation, she didn't have enough courage to listen to his answer. She kept her reply short and off the subject.

"Eric has the granola on the table."

"Oh." Tony looked over his shoulder toward his nephew. "Thanks. Hey, shortstuff, you better go get your school clothes on. Tell Christina we're leaving here in ten minutes."

"Okay, Uncle Tony." Eric got up from the table, his last piece of jelly toast in his hand, and ran over to wrap himself around his mother's legs. "I missed you, Mom."

Jessica leaned down and kissed his honey-blond head. "I missed you too, sweetheart. We'll do something fun together on Saturday, just you and me, so think up some ideas. Okay?"

"Okay, Mom." He raised his face to give her a toast-crumb-and-jelly kiss on the cheek.

After he'd left the kitchen, she looked over and caught Tony's eye.

"I'm sorry about last night," she said.

He shrugged. "Not as sorry as your boss will be if anything happens to you or one of the kids because of his business problems."

"I should have known better than to bring the woman home."

"I'm not sure you had much choice, Jessie. She was sick, exhausted, and she wouldn't go anyplace else. Sometimes we have to make decisions we'd rather not have to make. This one should turn out okay. When I called Luke last night, he started a quiet investigation to have Cao Bo checked out from Immigration to Chinatown. If anything turns up, he'll be on it."

Jessica nodded her thanks. Their oldest brother, Luke, was a detective with the San Francisco Police Department, with enough years behind him to have a net of connections stretching across the Pacific Rim. If Cao Bo had brought trouble with her, Luke would find out about it.

"I'll call him later to see if he's come up with anything," she said.

"Okay, Jess. There's one other thing."

"Yes?"

"About John Liu and Yuxi. Why did you have Cooper bring them in? You know nothing could happen around here that you and I and Paul can't handle."

"I know. I just thought we'd all be safer with another line of defense in the house."

"We," he asked, "as in you, me, Paul, and the kids? Or we as in Cooper Daniels?"

Jessica took a sip of coffee, hiding behind her cup and wondering if she had any secrets left at all.

"Well, Jess?" Tony pushed for an answer to his question.

"He's in trouble," she admitted. "He needs help, and I'm not the only one who thinks so."

"I would hate to see you get hurt," Tony said, his voice growing soft and his eyes looking wiser than their years.

"Me too."

"Do you care that much?"

"I shouldn't," she said, lowering her gaze.

She heard him rise from the table and walk across the kitchen floor. He stopped and gave her a quick hug on his way out, but she couldn't tell if he was giving her support or consolation.

She definitely felt like she needed both. Cooper had done nothing but aggravate her and set her off from the first moment they'd met, and drive her crazy with illicit imaginings. She could hardly look at him without thinking about the way she'd first seen him— naked—and thinking about him naked made her think of a whole lot of other things.

With a subdued sigh, she tore off a paper towel and used it to wipe the jelly off her cheek. One look at her legs confirmed that she would need to wash her jeans to get the fruit and butter off them.

It was Monday morning, and despite a near-irresistible urge to crawl into bed and not surface for a week, she downed the last of her coffee and braced herself to meet the day.

# NINE

By the time Jessica got herself to work, it was well after noon. She closed the Daniels, Ltd. door behind her and was immediately aware of the sound of the shower running in Cooper's private office. Calming herself with a deep breath, she walked over to turn on her desk lamp. The morning's sunshine had been consumed by a heavy bank of fog rolling in from the Pacific. She had been the last one out of the house, and was apparently the last one to arrive at the office.

Cooper was in there naked again. She set her purse on the floor and lowered her face into her hands, shaking her head. What was she going to do with him?

Hand him a towel?

Offer to soap his back?

Beg him to please not take his clothes off in the office anymore, because her heart couldn't take it?

She was overreacting. She always overreacted when

he was naked, or when he kissed her. She needed to get a grip.

Dragging her head up with a sigh, she walked to the dragon doors and closed them in the name of discretion and normal blood pressure. He could come out when he was decent.

When she turned back to her desk, she realized she wasn't alone.

"Hello." A man was sitting in the wingback chair by the window, his voice deep and calm, with a faint Scottish burr.

Startled by his presence, she barely managed a reply. "Hello."

"George didn't do you justice," the man said, rising from the chair. He was dressed in an impeccable gray suit, which he wore with the air of a man whose clothes were always tailored to perfection and of the highest quality. His dark blond hair was neatly trimmed. His demeanor was one of perfect control.

"I beg your pardon?"

"Forgive me," he said with a half smile of apology. "I'm Andrew Strachan. We were supposed to have met in London, and no doubt would have if Cooper hadn't gotten overly possessive."

"Oh, Mr. Strachan, of course." She stepped forward and offered her hand.

"Cooper and I have some unfinished business related to the Hawaiian fiasco. I hope he's not planning on bathing the rest of the afternoon."

Andrew Strachan was very smooth and self-assured,

but underneath his calm exterior and easy smile, she sensed a wealth of displeasure.

"Fiasco?"

"Pablo Lopez," he said. "The deal you contracted with George. Cooper didn't come through. I'm here to find out why."

She was stymied for an answer. When she'd asked Cooper about Hawaii, he'd told her everything had gone according to plan. Obviously, his plan had been different from the one he'd asked her to negotiate.

It would have been nice if he'd told her the truth, she thought. Then she wouldn't look like such a fool to Andrew Strachan.

"I'm sure Mr. Daniels will have an explanation. If you would care to be seated, I'll let him know you're here."

"Don't bother. Cooper has a sixth sense when it comes to me and his women." Strachan's smile curled higher. "Believe me, he's probably already figured out that I'm here."

Stymied again, and flustered at being referred to as Cooper's woman, she did the one thing she'd sworn she would never do again the rest of her life: She asked a professional equal if she could get him a cup of coffee.

"That won't be necessary," a familiar voice said behind her, before Mr. Strachan could decide for himself.

"Cooper." Strachan gave a short nod.

Jessica half turned, not knowing what to expect, and found her boss practically dressed. His plaid shirt was still mostly open while he worked the buttons, but his jeans were zipped, and he was wearing shoes.

"Andrew." Cooper finished with the buttons and began tucking the tails of his shirt into his pants. That's when she noticed the jeans weren't snapped, and that his belt wasn't buckled. With his hair wet and slicked back off his face, he made an enticingly provocative picture of a man fresh from his shower. She couldn't look at him without remembering how close they'd been and what they'd done on her couch. Color rose in her cheeks, embarrassing her even further.

"My men told me Lopez wasn't where he was supposed to be yesterday," Strachan said. "Did we have a misunderstanding? Or did he make you a better deal?"

"He got away." Cooper shrugged, finishing with his pants, and walked over to the coffee machine set up on an antique credenza next to Jessica's desk. "You got some of your merchandise back. That's more than you usually get."

"Not much merchandise," Strachan countered, then added, "I'll take mine black."

Cooper poured three cups and offered them all around. "I looked in the warehouse where Lopez had it all stockpiled. There must have been at least fifty tons of the *Callander*'s cargo still in salable condition."

"Minus your commission, of course."

"Of course."

Strachan sighed and pulled a thin cigar out of the breast pocket of his suit. "Do you mind?" he asked

Jessica. When she shook her head, he turned back to Cooper. "What am I going to do with you, Cooper?" His tone made his disappointment clear.

"Pay me."

Glancing at Cooper, Jessica saw he wasn't the least bit concerned with Andrew Strachan's disappointments.

"It's a possibility," Strachan said, then bent his head and lit the cigar he'd put in his mouth. After drawing deeply and exhaling a cloud of smoke, the Scots wolf met her boss's unwavering gaze.

" 'Possibility' covers too many options, Andrew," Cooper said. "You only have one. Eight percent."

Strachan smiled, a wolfish grin conceding defeat. "Three percent."

"Five."

"That's only a fraction of what Somerset agreed to pay you for Lopez," Strachan pointed out. "Why did you let him go?"

When her boss didn't reply, Strachan spoke again. "I'm worried about you, Cooper. I think you're going to get yourself hurt, and Jackson wouldn't have wanted that to happen."

"Your bank knows where to send the money. I'll give you a week to make the deposit."

"Whatever Lopez traded you for his life is going to be what gets you killed."

"You should have more faith in me, Andrew."

Jessica felt the confrontation come to an uncomfortable draw, with Strachan being the first to lose control of his temper.

"Baolian isn't some simple bitch with nothing better to do than kill off bounty hunters." The cigar left a trail of smoke in the air from Strachan's abrupt hand gesture. "The word out says she wants the Daniels name wiped off the face of the earth. Why? What did you do to her, Cooper?"

"That's between me and Baolian," he said.

"I warned you not to get personally involved," Strachan said, his voice low and serious. "I warned you what she was like."

"We were never *personally* involved." Cooper's jaw grew tight with anger. "She wanted Jackson, and when Jackson didn't want her, she wanted him dead. Well, she got what she wanted, and it's going to cost her more than she's willing to pay."

With a disgusted snort, Strachan stepped forward to the desk and crushed his cigar into a pristine cloisonné ashtray. "You'll never hurt her badly enough to make up for what she did." He lifted his head and looked directly at Jessica. "Reason with him. I'd rather not lose two close friends in the same year."


"Crown jewel," Jessica muttered, flipping through the computer printouts and notes she'd been compiling for three days. With Cooper's weeks of intensive research and years of knowledge, and Cao Bo's new information—which included all of Fang's Western Hemisphere properties, businesses that were so deeply hidden, it would have taken Jessica two years to find them—Jessica had an extensive list of Fang Baolian's holdings. But she had not been able to find anything even remotely resembling a crown jewel.

Neither had she been able to reason with Cooper. Strachan's warnings had not fallen completely on deaf ears. She'd heard every word and taken them to heart. But nothing was going to stop Cooper in his quest for revenge.

She had discovered that Baolian's favorite port was Manila, but the pirate actually did more business out of Hong Kong. She knew the Dragon Lady lived on a phantom ship now named *Sea Cloud*, a floating palace that plowed the waters of the South China Sea. She did not know what it would take to entice the pirate off her ill-gotten home and into Cooper Daniels's clutches, or what he would do to Baolian once he had her. She didn't want to know.

Laughter from Cooper's office stopped her in the middle of flipping a page. Cao Bo had not gone away, or home, or back to whatever boat had brought her to California's shores. She had gone to Cooper's house.

Straightening her shoulders, Jessica forced her thoughts back to the work at hand. Cao Bo wasn't her concern. Lots of people lived at Cooper's house, John Liu for one, Yuxi for another.

And Cooper.

And Cao Bo.

"Damn," she whispered, turning back a page to pick up where her thoughts had trailed off.

He was being nice. The same way she had been nice to the young woman. It was the least Ms. Cao deserved. Without her information, Jessica wouldn't have half of the facts she'd been working with all morning. Without Cao Bo, she wouldn't have known of Baolian's connections to a small herb shop in San Francisco's Chinatown. With assets well under ten thousand dollars, it was a virtual nonentity in the pirate's portfolio, which only increased its importance.

What was a multimillionaire doing with a tiny herb shop in the States? That was the question Jessica was trying to answer. That and what in the world did she think she was doing hunting pirates. She liked to tell herself it was a good-paying job, but her conscience wouldn't accept the lie. She was in up to her ears with tankers, freighters, and merchant vessels, because Cooper Daniels had kissed her.

The deep laughter came again, and she gave up the pretense of work. She couldn't concentrate with the two of them in there laughing. Cooper had never laughed with her about anything.

Standing, she smoothed her skirt and checked her watch. It was lunchtime, the perfect excuse for finding out what was going on in his office.

There were a few things she questioned about Ms. Cao, not the least of which was her most opportune appearance. Luke had yet to come up with anything suspicious beyond Bo's illegal status, but Jessica still felt uncomfortable with the younger woman. She wasn't alone in her feelings; Bo herself was uneasy with everyone. Her discomfort showed in her silent alertness and the way she always kept a certain distance between herself and other people in a room, as if she was afraid someone might try to grab her.

They didn't know where she'd come from or who had sent her, or what her motives were for giving them so much information. That she was in someone's employ was a reasonable assumption. That her employer continued to remain anonymous was unsettling. A loose end of such profound proportions could prove to be dangerous. They had expected Bo's employer to show his hand by now, to request a favor in payment for the information. Jessica hoped granting that favor wouldn't be the final burden to crush Daniels, Ltd., or get Cooper killed.

She knew Cooper also felt the inherent, blind obligation in accepting Bo's help, but he was more than willing to take a risk if it could get him what he wanted.

She stood before the closed office doors, suddenly reluctant to open them and face Cooper. He should never have kissed her, especially to the point of combustion. And he most certainly should never have stopped kissing her. For the first two weeks she'd worked there, nary a soul had shown up at Daniels, Ltd. Since the dragon had taken up residence, the office had turned into Grand Central Station. They hadn't had one quiet moment together since Sunday night on her couch. Even those rare times when the stars had aligned to give them quiet and a moment, Bo was always there, or John, or Yuxi, or any number of other less savory characters who came in to sell information.

He was driving her crazy. Her situation was untenable. She didn't know how she was going to walk away from him, and the mess he was in, on Friday, but she had to find a way.

Until then, she had a responsibility to do her job, and her job included finding out what in the hell they were giggling about in the next room.

After a perfunctory knock, she opened the dragon doors, hardly giving the fierce beasts a second glance. Cooper and Bo were not alone as she'd thought, and it wasn't Cooper laughing with the young woman. John and Yuxi must have arrived via the private elevator, because they were in the room, setting out lunch and talking to each other in what Jessica now recognized as Cantonese. Both men were laughing, but John was looking at Bo with a teasing expression. He spoke again, his voice soft and imploring, and his effort elicited a shy response.

Jessica could tell by the color blooming on Bo's cheeks that she thought Chinese-American men were very forward.

"Ms. Langston," John greeted her as she entered. "Your and Cooper's lunch will be ready in a moment. Yuxi and I will be taking Ms. Cao out to eat."

The man knew how to get a startling amount of information across in very few words. She and Cooper were having a private lunch together, an important lunch if he was relinquishing the responsibility for Ms. Cao's safety. Not that John Liu didn't look more than capable of handling anyone who tried to grab the woman.

She looked over at Cooper and caught his eye just as he turned away. He was standing by the large window overlooking Powell Street and the Bay beyond. Sunlight illuminated his profile and cast golden highlights in his hair and along the curve of his cheekbone. His mouth was grim, his jaw tight, and Jessica suddenly felt selfish for resenting the thought of his laughing with another woman. If she was smart, and she was beginning to have her doubts that she was, he'd be doing a lot more than laughing with another woman. He needed some sort of comfort, some easing away of the stress drawing lines in his face. He needed a soothing touch, and more and more, she wanted to be the one to give it.

In an act of pure self-defense, she forced her gaze back to John and the lunch. Cooper Daniels was not for her. She couldn't make the facts any plainer to herself. Green-eyed dragons living on the edge of danger did not make suitable companions for mothers of growing children, no matter how incredibly they kissed.

John set a delicate porcelain teapot on the low table next to a bottle of chilled white wine and pulled silk cushions out from underneath, arranging them to make comfortable seating. Next came two sets of finely made chopsticks with their tiny porcelain rests.

Jessica watched the careful preparations with growing dismay.

Silk cushions and privacy automatically, and much to her embarrassment, made her think of sex, or at least of kissing. Cooper Daniels had given her a one-track mind.

When the last dish was set out, John rose from the

floor and went over to speak privately with Cooper. With Cooper's quiet dismissal, they all left, and Jessica noticed that neither John, nor Yuxi, nor Bo stepped on the dragon, not so much as an accidental tweak of an ear or a shoe scraping against a bronze scale.

Taking their carefulness as a sure sign that there was an ancient Chinese proverb detailing the ills that befell those who trampled dragons, she was glad she'd always been equally careful—except for that once when her foot may have skimmed the dragon's nose.

The dragon posing the more immediate danger stepped away from the window then, drawing her attention back to the problem at hand: eating lunch with Cooper Daniels while lounging on a pile of silk cushions and keeping her hands to herself.

"Have you come up with anything?" he asked, circling behind his desk with a lazy grace at odds with the grimness of his expression. His limp was still present in his walk, but it was far overshadowed by the deliberateness of his movements. Every muscle in his body was responding as if on cue, fluid and charged with energy.

He was on the prowl. She felt it as surely as she was standing there. She watched him pick up an envelope and glance at the return address before tossing it aside. In the next heartbeat, she was captured and held by his glittering gaze.

"Well?" he asked, his voice devoid of any polite modulation. He was angry and tense, and neither state was hidden. Unlike herself, she realized, the man did not have kissing on his mind.

She knew what he wanted—the same impossible thing he'd wanted her to give him all along, the edge on Fang Baolian. No pirate hunter had ever succeeded in getting close to the dragon lady. No one had ever gotten the best of her.

"There's a small business, an herb shop on Grant Street," she said, "that doesn't fit her portfolio. It's not big enough to launder a significant amount of cash, but she could be running some money through it." She knew it wasn't much, but it was all she had to offer.

"What about Singapore? Jakarta? Hong Kong? Manila?" he asked, naming Baolian's bases of operation.

"She doesn't have a big enough piece of the Jakarta project for it to be a crown jewel. As far as anything else in the Far East is concerned, I think there's too much risk for too little chance of success on her home ground, unless you're willing to spend a year or more getting someone inside her organization. At that point, your options would be limitless. You could run your own investigation into her underground financial structure, and could probably get any number of governments interested in commandeering a fair share. You could sabotage her pirating runs, or embezzle her into bankruptcy. Extortion might work, providing there is anything such as honor among thieves. I, of—"

"There is," he assured her, interrupting as he came around the side of his desk.

"I, of course," she continued, "will not be involved in those decisions."

She watched as he picked up a folder from his desk and crossed his office. His footsteps stair-stepped the crenellations of the dragon's back with impunity. He walked on and over the snapping furl of the dragon's tail and stopped on the cream-and-gilt-encrusted breast scales that would have covered the dragon's heart, if such a beast had a heart.

"There's a name in here," he said, handing her the folder. "The man is a banker on Grand Cayman. It's what saved Pablo Lopez's life."

"I'll see what I can find out." She accepted the folder with only the slightest hesitation.

"Do you believe in what I'm doing?" he asked.

"I understand revenge. I'm not sure I sanction it."

"Do you think I'm going to get revenge?" One dark eyebrow lifted as he spoke, adding the dragon's own edge to his question. After a moment of her silence he moved closer, bringing a wash of tension with him across the room. He stopped near enough for her to see the streaks of turquoise darkening the subtler green of his eyes.

"You're going to get something," she said, measuring her words against the sudden quickening of her pulse. "Maybe revenge. Maybe yourself killed. I'm not sure which."

"Will you miss me when I'm gone?"

"That's a terrible question."

He lowered his lashes for a second, as if agreeing with her, then his gaze was back on hers, intense and inquiring, and his voice softened.

"Will you kiss me?"

His question was straightforward. Her reaction was a maelstrom.

Her palms dampened and her mouth went dry. A curling sensation wound down through her stomach, heightening her awareness of her body and the closeness of his. Warmth radiated off him along with tension, acting like a magnet to draw her nearer. She closed her hands into fists, resisting the urge to reach for him, to give him the caress he'd asked for.

"Please?" His voice was husky as he moved a step closer. His hand came up to stroke her cheek. "Chow Sheng was right. You have beautiful skin."

His gaze trailed over her face like a touch, making a path for his fingertips to follow. This was the soothing he needed, the soothing she longed to give—a kiss, a caress. He lowered his head close to hers, resting his cheek on hers before sliding his mouth down the side of her neck. He came back up the same way with exquisite slowness, making every moment last. His breath blew against her skin as he spoke.

"Open your mouth for me, Jessie . . . kiss me." He stopped just short of the deed, making it unbearably easy for her to rise on her toes and turn her face a bare inch to find his lips. She was lost.

She tasted him with her tongue, a tentative foray beginning at the corner of his mouth and following the full curve of his lower lip. A sigh of satisfaction rumbled up from deep in his chest, but he did no more than tighten his arm around her waist and pull her against his pelvis. The kiss was hers to initiate, a task that became easier and easier with the increase in contact between their bodies. Where they touched, there was heat. Where he moved against her, there was meltdown.

His anger hadn't abated. It had been changed, refocused, been transformed into need.

Her eyes closed on a soft exhalation, and her arms slid up his chest and around his neck. She wanted to savor him, explore him. She touched her mouth to his and felt his breathing slow. Her lips parted and pleasure suffused her senses.

This was the kiss Cooper had wanted. Her tongue laving the inside of his mouth and filling him with a hunger for more. Her giving instead of just accepting, a kiss without tears.

She molded herself to him, and the soft crush of her breasts against his chest made his gut tighten. He slanted his mouth over hers to deepen the kiss and take them both higher. She was his. She felt so right, too right not to be his. He rubbed himself against her and groaned with the pleasure the simple act gave.

The timing was dead wrong, but his feelings were undeniable. He wanted to make love to her, sink himself inside her and lose himself in the sweet mystery of her. She was beautifully female, all giving softness with a seductive power he didn't even attempt to resist. He wanted her to take him.

With that goal in mind, he slid his hands down her hips and began inching up her skirt. He got the hemline up about an inch and a half before her hands covered his and stopped his little adventure.

"This is going to happen," he murmured against her mouth.

She didn't deny him; she only kissed him and kept kissing him. The skirt came up another inch.

"Damn." He stopped himself, then swore again. "But it isn't going to happen here, and it isn't going to happen now. How in the hell do you do it?"

"Do what?" she asked, her voice breathless in a way that made him wish something *was* going to happen.

"Make me into the gentleman I most certainly am not," he said, thoroughly disgusted with his attack of virtue.

He pulled back far enough to see her eyes, and she did the damndest thing. She grinned at him. He would have laughed at the sheer audacity of it, if he'd been in any condition to laugh.

# TEN

Lunch was strained, and Jessica knew Cooper was making darn sure she knew why. She'd grinned at him with pure satisfied delight, enjoying her back-handed victory over him—and she'd been paying the price ever since.

"Have you ever made love on a pile of silk pillows spread out on top of a dragon?" he asked, reaching for another shrimp-and-coconut delicacy. His gaze flicked over her. "You can take that any way you want."

"No. I have not, in any way." She watched him pick up the crustacean with his chopsticks, refusing to meet his eyes. She had progressed far beyond blushing. She didn't think anything more he said could shock her.

He leaned over and whispered in her ear, and her face warmed to a rosy hue.

"You're scandalous and . . . and . . ." She gave up in frustration. She didn't know what else he was, so she busied herself with moving food around on her plate. The lunch was haute cuisine, but she hadn't put anything in her mouth yet that was even close to tasting as good as he had tasted. If he hadn't stopped of his own accord, the silk-and-dragon issue would have been a done deal, and they both knew it.

The kiss had hit her like a bolt of lightning. She still hadn't recovered her equilibrium, which was why he was getting away with his outrageous conversation. He'd turned physical foreplay into verbal foreplay. She was incapable of resisting either.

"Wanting to take your clothes off is hardly scandalous, Jessie. You're driving me crazy and have been ever since you walked in my door," he said, not sounding any too happy about the fact.

She'd seldom heard anyone talk so seriously and openly about sex. He wasn't teasing her, and he sure as hell wasn't flirting. He meant every word he was saying, but no matter what he said, wanting to see how far he could get taking her clothes off with his mouth was scandalous.

"You were angry when I walked through your door," she corrected him.

"I was naked."

Her blush deepened. She was floundering. He was more than she could handle—physically, emotionally, or verbally. "That wasn't my fault either."

"I'd be happy to give you a shot at making my nakedness your fault." He helped himself to noodles and gave her a quick, sardonic grin she pretended not to see. "Every time you kiss me, I get the idea you'd know just how to go about it, and as we've already ascertained, I've got a hundred ways I'd like to do it to you."

It was impossible for her blush to deepen, so it spread. Jessica knew she was supposed to like her body—every feminist said so—and she was proud of the two children she'd borne and nurtured, but getting naked with Cooper Daniels would be a tricky move if she wanted to keep her ego intact.

"We're not really . . . uh, right for each other." She hadn't wanted to voice the obvious, but somebody had to keep things in perspective.

"I know," he said, cocking his head and giving her a wry look. "But that doesn't seem to be making a hell of a lot of difference in how I feel."

She knew exactly what he meant, and she knew it meant trouble.

"I'll be gone in two days," she said.

"If I thought it would change your mind about what we should do with the afternoon, I'd fire you right after lunch. But I don't think our job association is the only barrier between me, you, and a pair of damp sheets."

"You're crude."

"I'm honest, and I want you."

No one had ever said that to her. Such honesty could be flustering, and darkly thrilling.

"I'm no expert," she said, trying to regain her perspective. "But don't most men use a more subtle approach?"

He laughed and turned back to his plate. "I'm not sure I've got enough time to do this subtly."

Alarmed, she looked over at him and found him gazing at her.

"If Baolian wanted you dead, she wouldn't be trying to buy you off," she said with conviction, as much for her own peace of mind as for his.

"Yeah," he agreed, his face sobering. "But I'm not going to be bought."

She went back to her lunch, though her appetite was long gone.

"So men don't come on to you?"

Of all the things he could have come up with to continue the conversation, nothing could have been better designed to exasperate her—and get her mind off his very serious situation.

"No, Cooper. Men don't come on to me." She faced him and lifted her bangs. "Can't you see the 'wife' and 'mother' signs branded on my forehead?"

"You're not married."

"No, but I was for long enough for the label to stick." She gave him a look that said the conversation was over, but he didn't take the hint.

"Lots of men find that especially attractive in a woman, her being married to someone else."

"In my experience, it's the other way around, with women finding other people's husbands especially attractive."

"Paul told me about Ian," he said.

"I don't want to talk about him with you." She set her chopsticks down and prepared herself for getting up and leaving. They had already crossed the bounds of propriety and professionalism, and if they talked about her ex-husband, they were going to cross the bounds of civility.

Cooper's hand on her arm stopped her getaway before she had a chance to move.

"If he's part of the barrier, he's going to get talked about."

"Don't try to analyze me, Cooper." The edge in her voice gave away more of her feelings than she had intended, but it was too late for a flippant reply.

A heavy silence fell between them, and she could swear she heard his jaw clench.

"I don't want to analyze you," he finally said. "I want to make love with you, and believe me, I wouldn't be telling you that if I didn't have a damn good reason for thinking you wanted the same thing. I'm not a fool. I don't go around setting myself up for rejection, and I sure as hell don't make a pass at every woman who catches my eye. But you—" He stopped, frustration getting the better of him. He was silent for a long moment, and when he continued, his voice had softened to a pained whisper. "But you make me forget, Jessie, and I want more."

She was frozen in place by his words, her heartbeat slowing to a dull throb. She ached for him, for what he'd lost.

He swore, one succinct obscenity, and rolled to his feet. Walking away, he swore again, the same harsh sound. She turned on her pillow to follow him with her eyes. He stopped in front of the window and raked his hands through his hair. The sun-streaked layers slipped through his fingers like falling silk, making her want to do the same, to touch him and feel the life of him in her hands.

"We've only known each other a week," she said, her voice as unsure as she suddenly felt.

He looked over his shoulder at her, and there was a resignation on his face, a sadness that reached out and quietly broke her heart.

"It's been a hell of a week," he said, and turned back to the view.

He needed love, physical love, but despite the yearning she felt, Jessica knew she couldn't be the one to give it to him. The sacrifice was too great, the cost too high. He would go on and either triumph over his nemesis or be killed, and the odds were very high on him getting killed.

"You're right," she said. "It's been a hell of a week. I'll do what I can with the Grand Cayman banker and write up my recommendation."

Cooper heard her move behind him, and with a certainty that forced him into action, he knew he wasn't ready to let her go.

She finished rising from the floor and brushed off her skirt. It was a floral cotton thing, kind of full, but elegant rather than casual with its black background and overblown cinnabar peonies. The matching blouse had a stand-up collar and buttoned down one side. It was the loops around the buttons that had made him think of taking her clothes off with his mouth.

She was beautiful. She'd kissed him with warmth

and passion, and talking with her about making love
had smothered his last polite instinct.

She began walking toward the door, and he swiftly
crossed the room to cut her off.

"I think you should concentrate your efforts on the
herb shop," he said. "The Chinese are very particular
about their herbs."

"There's not much there to concentrate on."

They both stopped at the door. Cooper put his
hand on the knob and wondered just how far he'd go
to keep her with him awhile longer. "I'll send John
this afternoon to check it out."

"Okay." Her lashes lowered. He could tell by the
hesitation in her movements that she wanted to say
something else.

"What, Jessie?"

"Maybe when all this is over . . ." She paused for
a deep breath and lifted her eyes to meet his gaze.
"Maybe then we could see each other."

"Why?" He asked the question softly, feeling a
rush of hope surge into his bloodstream. Quickly on
hope's heels came another dose of frustration. He
didn't want to wait until anything was over. When
everything was over, he'd probably be over too. God,
if Baolian didn't get him, another cutthroat probably
would. He'd pushed himself so far out on a limb, he
couldn't even see the damn tree anymore. He'd called
in favors and twisted arms that were used to doing the
twisting. He'd all but put his soul in hock to people
who wouldn't hesitate to claim it if he didn't come
through for them.

She faltered for a second, obviously caught off guard by his directness. Then she surprised him.

"Because you fascinate me," she answered, "and every time you kiss me, I feel something I've never felt before. I want to find out what it is."

He hadn't expected such honesty.

"Part of it is lust," he said, feeling compelled to match her honesty with his own.

"And the rest of it?" she asked.

"Part loneliness," he admitted, knowing that particular truth didn't put either of them in a very noble light.

"There's still something more." She sounded convinced, and he didn't dissuade her. He believed it too.

"Yes. There's something more, and I'm no more sure of what it is than you are. But I—"

He was interrupted by someone's noisy entrance into the reception area. Their eyes held for a second, then he moved a panel hidden in the elaborate carving of the dragon door and looked through a secret peephole.

"Chow Sheng has arrived with two of his guards," he told her. "Stay here until he leaves. I don't want him getting any more ideas about you."

Jessica stepped back and watched him leave, realizing she'd just made a fatal error. She'd told him the truth about her feelings. The enormity of her stupidity made her groan.

Jessica kept a vigil at the dragon door for over half an hour before she left her post to put together a snack off their lunch table and to pull a chair to the door so she could get off her feet. The conversation had alternated between English and Cantonese, with enough of her mother tongue used for her to have learned the reason for Chow's imperious disregard for Cooper's privacy and time.

Cooper owed him money. Lots of money. Chow had come to suggest Cooper reconsider Baolian's offer, using the threat of calling his loan as an incentive for Cooper's cooperation.

Cooper had countered with a threat of his own: to tell Fang Baolian that her lackey dog had given money to the enemy, to pad the enemy's war chest against his mistress.

Chow had blanched at Cooper's words, and made it very clear that he and Baolian were nothing more than business associates, for only a mad monkey-dog would enter the jade gate of a dragon whore, which, it was said, had more teeth than a jackal. Chow had said all of this in English, wanting to make sure, Jessica surmised, that Cooper understood every single word.

As to Cooper's threat, Chow had been unimpressed. Fang Baolian preferred her business associates to have power over her enemies, he'd told Cooper, and it had been such a worthless amount of money. Even Cooper must be able to see that Chow had not endangered the empress of the South China Sea. If anything, he had done her a favor by indenturing her enemy to himself with the loan.

Jessica's heart and hopes had sunk with every

revelation. Cooper's ship was taking on water at an alarming rate. He was sure to go down.

But he hadn't taken Chow's offer. Baolian had doubled her payoff, and still Cooper had held firm. Jessica had always thought she admired men with principles, but she was afraid watching a man die for his principles would greatly change her appreciation for the art of compromise.

"Damn you, Cooper." She picked up a shrimp, then let it fall back onto her plate when the phone rang, startling her. Before she could make a move to answer it, the ringing stopped. She checked the outer office and saw Cooper speaking into the receiver.

Thinking how awkward it might be for him if the caller was delivering vital information, she debated if she should get on the other line, then decided he could handle the situation without her resorting to possible rudeness. She reached for the shrimp again. Again she returned it to the plate. Her stomach was growling, but it was in a tangle of knots that precluded eating.

Tucking her feet under her on the chair, she leaned on the padded arm and looked back through the peephole, only to discover things had changed in the other room—dramatically. Her body stiffened and the plate slipped to the floor unnoticed.

John Liu and Cao Bo were just returning, and their entrance sent instantaneous shock waves through the reception area. A moment's more dallying with the shrimp, and Jessica would have missed the most important exchange she'd seen since she started working for Daniels, Ltd.

If Chow Sheng had blanched at the mention of Baolian as his mistress, he turned absolutely bloodless when Cao Bo walked into the room. His dark, slanted eyes widened into perfect *O*'s, and his long-nailed fingers fluttered over his heart, as if he could contain the shock that organ had just received. As quickly as he'd fallen apart, he pulled himself together, turning his face aside and speaking to one of his guards.

For her part, Cao Bo dropped her cloak of shy insecurity. When she saw whom she'd walked in on, her immediate reaction of fear was eclipsed by defiance. Her slight shoulders drew back and a challenge glittered in her amber eyes.

The whole exchange happened within the space of a breath, before Cooper could turn from the telephone, before John got all the way in the door, but the impact of it stunned Jessica. She swore softly, a word she'd never used but appreciated now for its earthiness.

In the reception area, much dissembling was taking place. Chow Sheng sedately informed his adversary of a prior appointment, assuring Cooper that their negotiations would be continued at a later date. No introductions were made, but John had drawn Bo close, as if she were a girl he was seeing and happened to bring with him to drop in on his boss. Yuxi inconspicuously placed himself in front of the couple and spoke in rapid-fire Cantonese, drawing all the attention in the room to himself.

Cooper looked disgusted with the unexpected turn of events and did his best to smooth things over and get Chow out of his office. The older man did not need any encouraging. He left in a flurry of silk robes and bodyguards, as if he hoped a speedy escape would absolve him of any repercussions from the chance meeting. That was the way Jessica read the situation, and she considered herself damn good at reading situations.

Her questions about Cao Bo tripled in the time it took for the outer doors to close behind the last bodyguard. Jessica understood the young woman's initial fear. The defiance was a different animal altogether. Defiance implied enmity, and enmity implied acquaintance. Chow Sheng and Cao Bo knew each other, and while Cao Bo may have been afraid of every other person she'd met in the last few days, she was not afraid of Chow Sheng. Quite the opposite, in fact. Chow Sheng was afraid of the young woman.

He was also afraid of Fang Baolian. The coincidence was not lost on Jessica.

# ELEVEN

The minute Chow Sheng was out the door, Jessica went into action. She ducked her head into the reception area and started giving orders.

"Yuxi, lock the door, please. John, will you come and secure the elevator? Make sure it won't move, then come back here to wait with Yuxi and Bo. Cooper, I need to see you in your office—alone." She ducked her head back behind the dragon doors, then popped it out again with a last question. "Does anybody have a firearm?"

All three men had turned toward her, and they nodded in unison. It was more backup than Jessica had expected, especially in the office. When Bo added her hesitant nod, she didn't know whether to feel additional relief or to give in to a stronger surge of dismay.

Dismay won. A glance at Cooper showed him having the same reaction. John was quicker than both of them, swinging the woman around and flattening her against the wall for a brief but thorough frisking. He came up with the handgun out of her tunic and gave Cooper an apologetic smile tinged with self-recrimination.

"Pretty women," he said with a shrug, as if there was no understanding them and he should have known better than to trust one.

Cooper agreed with both sentiments with a slight lifting of his brows.

Yuxi stayed with Bo as the rest of them went into Cooper's office. After securing the elevator, John returned to the reception area, leaving the two of them alone.

"General Langston, I presume?" Cooper said dryly, striding toward the table and the half-empty wineglass he'd left there.

Jessica ignored the sarcasm. She was too concerned with how to approach him with what she thought she knew.

"Nice little disaster we just had out there," he said, the idleness of the comment belied by the tightness of his jaw. He picked up his glass and tossed off the contents in one swallow.

"That wasn't a disaster, Cooper. That was a godsend," she said.

His gaze narrowed on her. "You've never struck me as the overly optimistic type. Do you want to explain your definition of a godsend?"

She wasn't sure just yet, and her uncertainty showed in her hesitation. "First I want . . . no. First I need to know what you're going to do with Fang Baolian."

"I thought that was apparent. I'm going to destroy her."

"Do you want to explain your definition of destroy?" she asked, throwing his question back at him.

He looked at her for a long moment, unnerving her with the intensity of his gaze. When he spoke, his voice was dangerously quiet.

"What do you know, Jessie?"

"I'm not sure."

"You were sure enough two minutes ago to cordon off the area and do a weapons check," he said, correctly interpreting her intent and her actions. "I want to know what was behind your decision."

She'd started the discussion. She was going to have to finish it, but she didn't have to give her knowledge away. "I need some guarantees."

Cooper stared at her. "Aren't you forgetting whose interests you are being well paid to keep in mind?"

"This isn't about money." She nervously clasped her hands together near her waist.

"What is it about, then, Jessie?"

"A woman's life," she said, then blurted out, "I don't want her killed. I don't want you to kill her." Jessica hadn't even known how important that truth was to her, until she'd realized she might hold the power to bring Baolian to her knees at Cooper's feet.

"Killing is her game, not mine," he said, lowering his gaze as he placed his empty glass back on the table.

"I don't believe you." She'd seen him with Chow

Sheng. She remembered the way he'd looked the first time she'd seen him—wild and capable of anything.

Anger darkened the eyes he slowly lifted to meet hers. "Fair enough," he said, not denying her accusation.

"You can ruin her financially, play any game you want with her assets, take her to the cleaners. I just don't want you to kill her." And that, she suddenly understood, was her bottom line. Her concern wasn't so much for Baolian's life as it was for Cooper's soul. With that flash of insight, Jessica knew she'd gone past the edge of lust, loneliness, and caring into—God, help her—love. It was the worst news she'd had all day.

"You're asking a hell of a lot," he said. "Are you sure what you've got is worth it?" The subtle warning in his tone told her she could push him too far.

"No," she said clearly, having no doubts that her answer was a shove in the wrong direction. But the stakes had gotten very high very quickly, and she couldn't afford to be anything less than honest with him.

Cooper felt all the tension of the afternoon go out of him in one moment of pure incredulity. She was fearless. There was no other explanation for her rash treatment of him and her total disregard for his suggestion of caution. He wasn't in the mood to be trifled with, yet she trifled with him at her leisure—and at her risk.

"I'm beginning to understand why I find you so damnably attractive," he said. It wasn't exactly a compliment, and he could tell by her reaction that she took the statement with the same ambivalence with which he'd given it.

"Tell me you won't kill her," she insisted once more.

"I won't kill her." The remark was deliberately offhand, deliberately devoid of sincerity. She was going to have to take a chance on him, because—so help him, God—he'd been taking an incredible chance with her. She'd gotten under his skin where he hadn't wanted anyone to be. She shook his carefully controlled sense of balance. She made him want, and he'd figured out within a week of Jackson's death that wanting was the precursor to pain. The more you wanted, the more pain you were setting yourself up to take.

"Okay," she said, letting out a long breath, apparently satisfied with his nonchalant guarantee. "I haven't got it all figured out yet, but something astounding just happened out in reception and I think it's the bait we've been looking for."

Cooper kept his silence and waited, still stewing over her high-handed approach.

"Did you feel anything happen when John and Bo walked in?" she asked.

*Feel?*

He thought for a moment, then said the only thing he could come up with. "No. I didn't feel anything happen. I felt anger, both at myself and at John for not being more careful."

"Well, I felt something happen."

"You were behind a solid oak door," he reminded

her, letting his skepticism show. "You weren't even in the room."

"I still felt it."

Okay, he thought, I'll bite. "Felt what?"

"Chow Sheng shaking in his boots."

"Slippers," he corrected.

"Whatever. He was the one who got caught in your office, not Cao Bo, and it scared him. She scared him."

"She scares me," he admitted, not seeing the problem.

"No, she doesn't, Cooper." She started toward the table, taking a quick sidestep around one of the clawed feet of the dragon woven into the rug. The movement was so subtle, so unconscious, Cooper doubted if she was even aware she'd done it.

Stopping next to one of the chairs, she rested her hip on the arm. Her voice took on an earnestness as she leaned forward. "What or who she might represent scares you, but *she* doesn't scare you. With Chow it's personal. She actually frightens him."

Cooper wasn't buying it. There were too many facts lined up on the other side. "Chow Sheng had two bodyguards with him, and Cao Bo probably doesn't weigh in at more than a hundred and five pounds soaking wet. I'm not convinced, Jessie."

"I'm not talking about on-the-spot physical violence," she said, sounding thoroughly exasperated.

"Blackmail?" he asked, though he wasn't sure how being seen in his office would provide anyone with leverage against Chow Sheng. When Cooper was in residence, many people came through his office, most of them with no pretense of friendship as their motive. People did show up to shake his hand every now and then and conduct a little business, and some people showed up simply to shake him down.

"No," she said, drawing the word out as she seemed to search for another. "Blackmail isn't quite right. It was more as if Bo had given him something he didn't want, something dangerous, like a scorpion nestled on a bowl of hibiscus."

She was inscrutable, Cooper thought impatiently, totally inscrutable—*like Fang Baolian.* The subtleness of Jessica's reasoning finally hit home, and his senses did an immediate shift from uninterested confusion to full alert.

"Who do you think she is?" he asked.

Jessica recognized the change in his attitude. He was taking her seriously. "I don't know, but my guess is that she's very important to Baolian, and part of what frightened Chow was knowing she was in the enemy's hands. He's going to try to take her."

She was right, and Cooper knew it down to his bones.

"Then the quicker we get her out of here, the better. Gather up any data you're going to need for the next couple of days." He strode toward the dragon doors. "We won't be coming back."

An hour later Jessica stood on a balcony overlooking the rugged coastline and stretch of beach between

Cooper's house and the Pacific Ocean. The house itself was not what she had expected as they'd driven north out of San Francisco. She'd expected redwood and glass, something with two or three stories, craggy and masculine. She'd gotten an oasis of white pine, wood floors, and stark simplicity all on one level and no larger than two thousand square feet.

An apartment over the detached garage belonged to John, while the house was built closer to the sea, with steps leading down to the beach. The cries of gulls filled the air, a strident avian backdrop to the more primal sound made by the ocean and the melody of the chimes hanging from the porch roof.

A gust of wind swept in from the sea and ruffled her hair. She absently pushed the strands back off her face and turned to go inside. Cooper hadn't brought her to his home to admire the view. They had work to do.

She headed toward the north wing of the house, where she could hear John and Cooper setting up the equipment they'd brought. On her way, she passed an open door and her steps slowed, her curiosity aroused.

Unlike the quiet sophistication of the rest of the house, the room looked like it belonged to someone who didn't know how to stop moving. Every sport she could imagine was represented by the appropriate equipment, from skiing—cross-country and downhill—to snorkeling and scuba diving. There were surfboards, tennis rackets, racquetball rackets, a hockey stick, old baseball mitts, a basketball, a mountaineering pack, and lengths of neatly coiled climbing rope next to a chalk bag. Underneath all the clutter was a futon, a television with a VCR, and a large wicker dresser. The stereo system was everywhere, with speakers placed in all four corners.

Jessica knew it was Jackson's room. The rest of the house was elegant, like the office where she worked. This room was exuberance and energy running amok, but it looked untouched, painfully quiet. The evidence of a life lived hard and to the fullest, but finished, made her all the more sad for Cooper. The place was a testament to what he'd lost, to the vitality that was no more.

Her gaze traveled the length of the room once again, taking in all the recreational equipment, the piles of movie videos and compact discs stacked here and there, and another realization struck her, startling her. Her brow furrowed as she stepped inside. Looking again with a more discerning eye, she walked around the room, carefully touching the things she discovered.

Her fingertips grazed a poster of a heavy-metal band. A matching T-shirt proclaiming their world tour lay on the wicker dresser. From the characters on the shirt, she surmised the concert had been heard in Japan.

An odd clay sculpture stood in one corner of the room and was being used as a hat rack. It was half tree, half man and poorly done. She knelt by the base and ran her fingers over the name etched into the glazed surface—Jackson. The accompanying date was less than a year earlier. A few feet away was another sculpture of exquisite quality and the same half-tree design, but with a woman's face and body. The name on it was Olivia.

On a wrought-iron bench pushed against the far wall were a number of photographs. One was of Cooper as she had never seen him, laughing wildly, with a glint of pure mischief in his eyes as he held a large half-eaten fish from a gaff. Next to him was a boy holding a somewhat smaller fish. But the smaller fish had the other half of Cooper's hanging out of its mouth. The boy's smile was pure innocence, all cocky pride and artless guile set off by a sly wink and a dark, silky ponytail.

The boy appeared again, a few years older, hair a little longer, in a number of the other photographs. One was a high-school graduation picture taken with Cooper by his side. Another, in which he had even longer hair, was with a young woman. She was tall and blond and willowy, dressed in a sequin-spangled minidress. He was in a tuxedo. The picture was signed: *To Jackson with love. Don't forget. Martha.*

Jessica picked up the photograph and brought it closer. This, then, was Jackson, she thought, not quite believing what she saw. He had been beautiful. No one could deny the appeal of the clean, sculpted lines of his face, or of his rakish smile, or of the sensuality of the ebony hair falling nearly to his waist.

The pictures proved what she had suspected. Jackson had been much younger than Cooper, young enough for Jessica finally to realize just how far Cooper would go to destroy the woman who had killed him.

Jackson had been more of a son to Cooper than a brother, or rather a half brother. The dark hair, a higher angle on his cheekbones, the deep rich green of his eyes, and the warm color of his skin bespoke a mixed heritage.

Jackson could actually have been Cooper's son, for all she knew. Cooper certainly had a penchant for beautiful Oriental women, and one way or another, he seemed to come in contact with quite a few.

She set the photograph down and let out a heavy sigh. If Jackson had been his son, she knew nothing would stop Cooper from exacting revenge, nothing short of his own death. For his sake, she hoped it wasn't so.

A change in the air, rather than any sound, warned her she was no longer alone. Her intuition told her who was watching. She'd been caught again.

Resigned to his anger, she turned around and was surprised and concerned to find his expression much more difficult to read. His face was a mask of stone, utterly blank.

"We're all set up and ready to go," he said. "I want you to research the name Pablo Lopez gave me, the man on Grand Cayman. Start with the banks. If you get a trace to anything in the U.S.A. that he's siphoning money back into, then we're in business. If Baolian has put a sizable portion of her assets in the States, it's because she's looking for a stable govern- ment and a capitalistic economy. If we find it, we've found her nest egg, her crown jewel."

He turned to leave, but her voice stopped him.

"Was he your son, Cooper?"

"No," he said gruffly, without moving to face her. "He was the son of Sun Yi and my mother."

"Who was Sun Yi?"

Even from across the room, she saw the telltale twitch of a muscle in his jaw, the cracking of his facade of indifference.

"Sun Yi was the man who loved my mother, but couldn't save her. He was also a pirate, running the biggest syndicate out of Hong Kong until he died and left it all to Fang Baolian."

# TWELVE

Dusk was edging across the eastern horizon and falling into the ocean before Jessica pushed away from her computer monitor. She stretched her arms above her head and rolled her shoulders, easing the strain of too many hours without moving. The room she was working in encompassed the whole north end of the house, giving her both the landward view and the beauty of the sunset in the west.

She'd been alone for at least an hour, maybe longer. Cooper had left so quietly, she hadn't known for sure when he'd gone. She hadn't seen John, Bo, or Yuxi since shortly after they'd all arrived. Cooper had given the men instructions concerning the security of the house and they'd gone, taking the woman with them.

Checking her watch, she decided it was time for her to go too. She made a quick phone call home and talked to the children and Tony. Paul was out for the evening, but her youngest brother had everything in hand. Jessica knew she had a lot to be grateful for when it came to the men she lived with. They felt their family responsibilities keenly and had welcomed her and the children with open arms. Arguments were inevitable, and more than once schedules had clashed and promises had been forgotten. After a tough first year, though, they had managed to find ways to air resentments and stay out of one another's space when privacy was more important than teamwork. The five of them now functioned more as a family than many regular families. Genuine love had grown between her children and their uncles, the kind of love that only came from sacrificing and putting work into a relationship.

Jessica was ever aware of what she owed her brothers, including—but not limited to—a lot of back rent and baby-sitting overtime. Her school loans were just coming due, and she still owed money on her divorce. In an amazing feat of legal sleight of hand, her adulterous ex-husband had fixed it so she actually owed him money on the property settlement. Debt wasn't crushing her, but only because Paul and Tony were holding the roof up over her and her children's heads.

The rest of her family had been able to offer moral support, but not much else. Her parents were retired and living on their pensions, and her other brothers had families of their own to raise.

Yawning, she pushed out of her chair and walked over to the oceanside windows. After a minute of watching the waves come in, she opened the glass doors leading to the balcony and stepped outside. The wind had dropped. The chimes were quiet.

She scanned the beach, looking for what she knew not until she saw him rising out of the darkening sea in a black wet suit. Water sloughed off his shoulders and streamed down his body, glistening and catching the colors of the sun. His face shone with the differing shades of the sky—gold where the light rimmed his profile, a darker bronze smudged to copper in the shadows.

Waves broke against his legs, foaming up his strong thighs and pushing him forward. The wet suit necessary to swim the north coast clung to him, accentuating the hard lines of his body. For all Jackson's exotic mystery, the younger brother had been no more beautiful than the man she watched. She reached for the balcony railing and closed her fingers around the weathered wood. Her breathing grew quiet and soft, and her pulse slowed, as if she'd come upon a wild creature easily frightened back into the liquid wilderness.

He slicked his hands back through his hair, pushing it off his face as he limped across the cooling sand. The tension that was so much a part of him seemed momentarily subdued, washed away by an elemental sea. Light and shadow played across the muscles in his arms, outlining the hard, rounded curves of his biceps and the corded strength flowing from shoulder to wrist.

Halfway to the stairs, he looked up and unerringly met her eyes. No smile graced his mouth. No acknowledgment was made other than the eternity that he held her gaze. Then he broke their silent contact and continued his walk to the house.

A shiver coursed down her spine, as if the wind had suddenly come back up. But there was no wind. There was only Cooper, mounting the stairs and coming for her. The truth hit her as strongly as it was unexpected and undeniable.

For a while she'd lost herself in her work. For a while she'd forgotten all the different ways he'd told her he wanted her.

He, she knew, had forgotten nothing. Every moment of his kisses flooded back through her senses and she felt an overwhelming urge to run. Yet she held her ground, allowing herself to remember, even though she knew her downfall would be in recalling how he made her feel.

Their lunch conversation returned to her mind verbatim, and heat burned through her. No man had ever taken so much as a bra strap off her with his teeth. It was definitely time to run, before he made it all the way to the balcony.

Still she didn't move, and she wasn't sure if it was politeness, fear, or anticipation that held her captive at the rail. If her decision had been based purely on desire, she probably would have slept with him on the massage table in his office approximately five minutes after she'd seen him, just long enough not to bother to say hello. The force of her attraction had been that strong.

Desire, however, wasn't enough to overcome her

trepidation. She didn't want to get hurt, and she sure as hell didn't want to get used.

"Hi," he said when he reached the top stair, and Jessica realized she hadn't moved so much as an inch in any direction.

"Hi. How was the water?" Her voice sounded stilted. Her body was frozen in place.

"Cold, but nice." A slow smile curved his mouth as he unzipped his wet suit. "Welcoming. Safe." He lifted a towel off the rail and used it to dry his arms and face. "Salty but sweet." A lambent light warmed his eyes when he looked up. "Cradling. Heavy with love for me . . . the way you could be."

The breath she'd been holding went out of her and her heart melted. He offered nothing more than the truth that he wanted her with a need he wasn't going to hide.

Moving closer, he lifted her hand in his and brought it to his mouth. He stroked his tongue across her palm before kissing her there, then placed her hand over his heart. His eyes came back to hers, and he waited.

His skin was cool where she touched him, his heartbeat a strong and steady rhythm echoing her pulse. A thousand reasons to say no fell over each other in her mind, and her body had a response for every one of them. She wanted to make love. But God, it was hard to let go.

She closed her eyes on a troubled sigh, hoping to come up with an answer. But no answer was needed, for he kissed her then, his mouth covering hers in a gentle but irrevocable act that claimed her for his own.

He slipped his tongue in her mouth with a soft groan and ran his hands down her body, cupping her buttocks and pulling her close. When she was pressed against him, feeling the dampness of his wet suit seep through to her skin, he slid his hands up under her arms and guided them around his neck.

She offered no resistance. Every move he made was too heavenly to resist, and deep down inside she knew the die had already been cast. They would make love. She would feel him on top of her, inside of her, infusing every pore of her being with his essence. She wanted nothing more. She would accept nothing less for the chance she was taking.

So she returned his kiss in full measure and let her hands explore the breadth of his shoulders and the sleek muscles of his chest.

"Don't stop there, Jessie," he said between kisses on her face. "Touch me."

She hesitated, then moved her hand lower, and he rolled his hips against her, and his voice whispered against her skin . . . *yes*.

She was totally seduced by his reaction and the feel of him sliding into her palm. There was a sensuality about him she'd never experienced with a man, a silent, compelling confession of needs, and the equally compelling admission that only she could meet them. The grace in his movements put pleasure above domination. Or so she thought until she felt her skirt fall to the deck. She'd been so consumed by his kisses, so fascinated with his arousal, the hardness and the responsiveness of him, she'd been unaware of where his hands had been or what they'd been doing.

She was still decent in her slip, but Cooper wasn't stopping with her skirt. His hands were already sliding up her blouse, unbuttoning her from the bottom up.

"Cooper . . . Cooper, what if the others—"

His fingertips grazing over the peaks of her breasts silenced her more effectively than a kiss. Sweet pleasure stole her breath and weakened her knees. He caught her to him with one arm around her waist, but his other hand continued to tease and tantalize, stroking her softly and slowly.

"Don't worry," he murmured. "No one is going to come within fifty yards of this house unless we're under fire." He kissed the side of her neck and bit the lobe of her ear. "John has Bo under benign house arrest at his apartment, and I sent Yuxi to your house."

That got her attention despite the sensual haze he was conjuring up.

"Why?"

She felt the muscles in his shoulder bunch and give with his shrug. "I wanted to get rid of him, and that seemed to be the place he could do the most good. I'll pick him up when I take you home." His hand tilted her chin so he could steal kisses off her lips. "Unless you'll stay here with me all night long"—he kissed her again—"and wake up with me in the morning?"

"I can't do that," she whispered, suddenly feeling unsure of what she was doing. She wanted to make love with him. She wanted to explore his body and partake of the pleasure he offered. But every time he spoke, his words told her he wanted more, and giving him more was exactly what she was afraid of.

"They'll be okay," he said, surprising her with the depth of his empathy, even though he'd misinterpreted her main concern. "I really did send Yuxi just to get him out of the house, but he was a police sergeant in Hong Kong before he immigrated. Nothing gets by him."

"I still can't spend the night," she said.

"I know. But you're spending the next hour making love with me. If I get lucky, maybe you'll spend two, and that's what I need most." He grew silent as he cupped her face in his palms and rested his forehead on hers. Silky-fine hair slipped over his brow and brushed against her cheek. With utter concentration, like a cat licking cream, he flicked his tongue over her mouth and lit her on fire.

She took the exquisite torture, until she was gasping and wondering what was coming over her. She'd never gasped from a kiss before. Then again, she'd never been simply licked before.

"Lord, I love how you smell, the way you taste," he murmured against her lips.

With no more than that, no more than the turn of a phrase and another soul-deep kiss, he made her reality disappear.

She slipped her hand farther into his wet suit and felt the powerful surge of his body's response. He swore softly, ever so softly, his hands tightening on her.

"Come with me, please," he said huskily, grasping her wrist and pulling her hand free. He twined his fingers with hers and, holding her tight, led the way to his room at the other end of the balcony.

A light headland breeze billowed the floor-length curtains covering the open doorway to his bedroom, the sheer pale material reflecting shades of the sunset. Inside, the air was warmer than outside, warm and inviting, like his bed with its plump white comforter draped partway on the floor, as if he'd only gotten out of the bed to bring her back into it.

"Let me undress you," he said, pulling her into the room and letting the curtains fall behind them.

"How?" she asked, somewhat wary and somewhat curious, remembering again what he'd whispered to her at lunch.

A quick grin teased his lips. "Not like that," he said, pulling her closer and reaching for the next button on her blouse. "That's a game for longtime lovers. Later we can work our way through the books, but the first time we make love isn't for playing around. Everything is too new. We're nervous."

"You're nervous?" she asked, her wariness decreasing.

His grin broadened, and the last of her buttons slipped free of its loop. "No," he admitted sheepishly. "You're nervous. I'm excited. But it amounts to the same thing. I've been thinking about you a lot, thinking about how it would feel to do this." He opened her blouse and carefully pushed it off her shoulders, letting it fall to the floor. "And this." His hands came back to her slip straps, his fingers sliding underneath and lifting them. He started to pull them down, but her hands came up to her breasts, stopping the aqua lingerie from going anywhere.

He quirked an eyebrow at her. "We're going a lot further than this, Jessie."

"Maybe." The word was a breath, her eyes wide and unsure.

Cooper had drawn some conclusions from the things Paul had told him about her marriage, and he had an idea of what the problem probably was. She hadn't been with a man in a long time, and as much as she wanted him, she had a lot of doubts, especially since the last man she had been with had been unfaithful to her. Adultery was hell on a person's self-worth and sexuality.

He hadn't been with a woman in a long time either, though his celibacy had more to do with dissatisfaction with casual sex than with any hurt he'd received. He had arrived at a time in his life where he only wanted one special woman. He hadn't been able to find her, until the totally inappropriate Ms. Jessica Langston had walked into his office. He didn't have any doubts with her.

Her importance to him didn't make sense in either the short run or the long run. She was a divorced mother living in the suburbs. She needed stability, commitment. He was a man living close to the edge of oblivion, and he needed her. Only her.

"I want to be careful with you," he murmured, smoothing his hands over her bare shoulders. "I don't want to push you too fast, or make you uncomfortable—but I also want to take your clothes off and lie down with you on my bed."

"Okay," she said, not sounding at all okay.

He took her at her word, giving her credit for knowing what she wanted even if she wasn't sure of how to go about getting it.

"You're very beautiful, Jessie." He traced the lace edge of her slip across the upper curves of her breasts and felt her quiver under his touch. A pleased smile curved his mouth. "You're voluptuous and soft, and I find that very erotic."

His hands skimmed lower, over her breasts and down her belly. Bunching her slip in one hand, he brought the material up above her hips and used his other hand to work her hose and underwear down. She grew very, very still.

"Don't stop breathing, darlin'," he drawled, "or this isn't going to be nearly as much fun as I thought."

"Don't tease me, Cooper. I'm a nervous wreck."

"If we can get all these clothes off, I think we can get beyond the nervous part pretty damn quick."

In silent agreement, she moved to help him, but balked again when it came to her slip.

"Not yet," she whispered.

"Then when?"

"I'm not sure." A soft blush colored her cheeks.

Unable to resist, he kissed the warmed skin. "All right, Jessie. I've got a plan. I'm going to take off my wet suit"—and he did, peeling it off his body with sure grace—"and take off your slip"—he did that too—"and then I'm going to put my hands all over you."

Without preamble or warning, he started with her most secret place, tunneling his fingers down through the triangle of soft curls between her legs. His eyes drifted closed on a ragged breath. God, she felt so good. He stroked her, feeling her woman's moisture dampen his fingertips and make his erection even stiffer. Whether she was unsure or not, her body was welcoming him, preparing to receive him.

"Lord, Jessie," he groaned. "You must have the willpower of a saint to be this wet and still say no. Either that or you're more innocent than I would have believed for a mother of two."

"Cooper?" she said breathlessly.

"Yes?"

"Let's not talk about the kids."

# THIRTEEN

Cooper took her suggestion to heart and stopped talking altogether, except to murmur encouragement. They stretched out on the bed, his body darkly golden and angular against her pale curves. He cupped her breast in one hand and massaged her nipple to a turgid peak while he kissed her, full of wonder at the beauty of her and the sweetness of her response. Her fingers combed languidly through his hair, and her breathing grew short and shallow, telling him of her pleasure.

When he lowered his head and took her in his mouth, her muscles tensed for a moment, then gave way completely in a melting surrender. She sighed his name and the sound went through him like a searing bolt of heat.

He kissed her everywhere, touched her everywhere, and with every kiss, every touch, his need for her grew. She offered oblivion, a focus and a driving need hot enough to consume him. He ached from wanting to be inside her, but the taste of her on his tongue compelled him to explore her feminine curves, to linger in soft, secret places made for the caress of his mouth.

When his brain started sending out warning signals, he moved up her body, blazing a trail of wet kisses, kisses meant to imprint her shape and the satiny texture of her skin on his mind. He kissed her where the sun had kissed her before, on her chest and shoulders and across the bridge of her nose, where a dusting of freckles graced her, and as he kissed her she began her own exploration.

She ran her foot up the back of his leg and down over his buttocks, teasing him, stroking him. Simultaneously she slid her hand down his chest and past his abdomen, tracing a double fuse line to his groin—then she lit it with her closing fist and a stronger stroking of his shaft.

Jessica felt his response build with every inch she traveled, until his body trembled with the need for control. When she reached her destination, he groaned and let her bring his arousal to a peak. Then he surged against her, swearing softly and making a crude request sound like an act of divine salvation. His breathing ragged, he nuzzled his head into the crook of her neck and whispered his request again. They were dark words, laden with primal fecundity, words meant to lure the innocent across the threshold of polite sex into a realm of pure, transcendent sensuality.

He pushed against her, breaching her silken sheath and sliding deep. Any illusions she'd had about what he wanted from her were shattered by the reality of his first thrust. He was gentle but unrelenting, burying himself to the hilt and then waiting as the exquisite pressure grew. His arousal throbbed deep inside her, heightening her excitement and bringing her closer to the edge of climax. He bent his head and licked her breasts before drawing a nipple into his mouth to suck and fondle with his tongue.

A gasp was wrung from her, and she clung to him, tangling her hands through his hair and holding him to her breast. Still he didn't thrust again.

She spoke his name, urging him on, near pleading with him, but he only brought his mouth to hers and whispered his request against her lips.

Dragons were a dangerous business, she realized. They were aggressive and demanding, and showed little sympathy for the faint of heart.

But they were also seductive, sensual creatures, ready and willing to push the envelope of her experience. He finally began a slow withdrawal, and her body convulsed around him.

"Cooper, no . . . don't." He pushed back inside, and her words changed to a soft moan. "Yes."

Her eyes fluttered closed and she raised her hips to meet him, taking the initiative, doing what he'd asked. She drew his head down to hers and opened her mouth to receive him. Matching him stroke for stroke, she was slowly engulfed in the sensual haze they created out of thin air and two bodies touching, skin to skin, and heart to heart.

She kept nothing for herself, no protection from the sweet lavings of his tongue, no inhibitions to hide behind. Her instincts were to cherish, to show him with her hands and mouth, and the welcoming gesture of her spread legs, how much she wanted him, how much he meant to her—Lord, what he was doing to her.

Cooper recognized every gift she gave, and he was awed that she gave so much. Her acquiescence was a haven, a safe place to let go of anger and forget guilt, a place of oblivion and succor. Her pleasure was a source of endless erotic stimulation. With every soft sound she took him higher. With every pelvic thrust she taught him a new and enthralling sensation. He couldn't get enough of her.

He levered himself up on his arms and gazed at the woman lying beneath him. Just looking at her made him feel tighter, harder. Her dark auburn hair was a tumble of soft strands across his pillow. The lines and curves of her body were an inspiration for the act of love, from the smoothness of her shoulders and arms to the gentle roundness of her belly. She was lithe and curvaceous like a female creature made to nurture. She was a woman and lovely, and he wanted her to have everything.

"Jessie, give me your hand." His voice was rough with strain. He hadn't meant to ask, he'd meant to do the deed and hope she'd follow his lead.

He had asked, though, and when she complied, lifting her hand with languorous grace, he smiled his pleasure. He was still embedded deeply within her, but the only movement he made was to bring her hand to his mouth and dampen her fingers. He swirled his tongue down over the sensitive tips and across her knuckles, and he felt her trembling contraction on his hard maleness.

With effort, he held his response in check. He was after more than release within her, and he was suddenly very sure he could get what he wanted.

When her fingers were wet, he slid her hand down over her belly and into the thatch of auburn curls between her legs.

"Touch yourself for me, Jessie," he murmured, guiding her in the act and watching the gentle gliding motion she made. Her thigh muscles tensed and her hips tilted higher. Her breathing grew labored. "You are so soft and sweet there. Let me—*Jessie* . . ." Her silken sheath tightened around him with agonizing pleasure, leaving him breathless.

He pumped into her, looking down and watching himself fill her again and again. She was coming apart in his bed, in his arms, and he wanted it to last forever. Even as the thought of forever came to life, a firestorm began building in his loins.

Jessica grasped the sheets with both hands, straining. Her legs came up around his waist, her ankles locking behind his back. Dragons were lovers. The strength of him overwhelmed her, the slickness of his movements and the heat of his skin. He was fire and energy, and he was taking her where she'd never been.

Cooper felt every muscle in his body coil in upon itself. He held off, knowing once he crossed a certain line there would be no control, no retreat, only the driving force of his body taking him to completion.

Her low moan and the surging of her body against him was the last thing he knew before the inevitability of climax claimed him. Her delicate contractions were made exquisitely powerful by the sensitivity of the shaft they milked. She convulsed around him, her inner walls rippling in counterpoint to the jetting of his lifestream. His back arched and he jerked against her, making it last, and last, until the final shudder ripped through him, leaving him dazed and struggling to find a steady breath.

He slowly lowered himself and cradled her in his arms, taking in a great gulp of air as he rolled her to his side. He'd known she'd be the death of him, but he sure as hell hadn't expected her to kill him in bed.

Sated, Jessica curled against her green-eyed dragon, inhaling the musky scent of man and the tang of the sea. He kissed her forehead and stroked her hair back off her face, touching her and soothing her still-trembling body. She wasn't sure what she and Ian had been doing all those years, but she'd never felt anything like what Cooper had given her. Luxuriating in the aftermath of his intensely beautiful lovemaking, she was ready to commit to him for life.

"You're dangerous," he said, his voice hoarse.

"*Moi?*"

"*Toi.*"

She looked up at him and he flashed her a wry grin. She hid her own smile against his chest.

"Are you sure you have to go home?"

She could tell by his tone that his grin had faded.

"Yes, I do," she said, tilting her head back to see him. "I'm sorry, Cooper."

Darkness had fallen since they'd first walked into his bedroom, but it wasn't dark enough to hide his disappointment.

"Then let me just hold you for a few minutes," he said, drawing her closer and tucking her head under his chin.

She sank against him, feeling his heartbeat under her palm and the strength of his arms around her. He twined their legs together. A heavy breath escaped him, sounding like a sigh of resignation, but he said no more. He only held her, letting the quietness fall and deepen.

When he knew he could keep her no longer, Cooper eased his arm from underneath her and helped her to her feet. He gave her a kiss before he let her go, but not the ravenous, sexual kisses he'd given her during their lovemaking. Tenderness and appreciation were his goals when he brushed his mouth over hers, gently rubbing her lips.

"I don't know how to tell you what happened to me when we made love," he said, still holding her close. "But I want more." He kissed her again and released her. "I'll get your skirt."

Jessica watched him leave, walking naked across the room and out through the door. The curtains blew around him for an instant before he disappeared.

She wanted more too, much more. For her sake even more than for his, she wished she could stay.

She wanted to wake up in his arms, without any time apart for her doubts to surface.

Jessica hadn't planned on being back at Cooper's house ready to go to work before he'd even gotten out of bed, but that's what happened.

John answered the door and let her in, and within minutes after she'd reopened her files in the makeshift office, he brought in a tea tray with croissants and fresh fruit.

An hour later Cooper still had not surfaced. Tempted as she was to go to his bedroom, Jessica refrained. John and Bo both had the run of the place, and she didn't want to be found in an unprofessional, compromising position with her boss. She very much wanted to be in an unprofessional, compromising position with her boss. She just didn't want to get caught in one.

Her doubts about what had happened between them had surfaced in spades, just as she'd expected. She'd forgotten to be embarrassed and shy the moment he had touched her, but she'd had the rest of the night and all of the morning to make up for lost mortification.

"Jessie?"

The sound of his voice brought her head around. He was standing in the doorway in a pair of plaid boxer shorts, his hair all tousled from sleep, his eyes drowsy with invitation, and his mouth curved in a purely wicked grin.

"Come on." He turned sideways in the door and held his hand out for her, beckoning. When she didn't move, he arched his brow.

It was the last bit of coercion he had to use the rest of the morning.


One and a half more days to survive, Jessica told herself that afternoon, then she could get a grip. She turned on her computer and tried to focus on the job at hand. She got as far as opening a file before a dreamy smile came over her, physically, emotionally, and mentally.

She'd made love with Cooper Daniels and left part of her heart in his bed, a bigger part than she could afford to lose. She wasn't an affair-type person, yet she'd made love with a man she barely knew—twice, maybe even more. She wasn't sure how a person counted the things she and Cooper had done. She did know the climaxes that had once been so rare in her life were starting to run together in her mind.

On a less rational side she felt as if she knew him very well indeed, like her own heartbeat. A ridiculous, romantic fantasy, she told herself, but the feeling persisted. She knew he would protect her with his life, that his courage could be counted on. She knew what had brought him his pain and that the loss was consuming him, guiding him down a path of certain destruction. If he lost against Baolian, he would lose all of the trappings of his life and maybe his life itself. If he won against the Dragon Lady, he would lose something else, something less easy to name but surely as important. And if he killed Baolian, he would kill part of himself.

She didn't think he understood the price his revenge would exact, and his lack of understanding compelled her to protect him. She was a mother. She knew the value of life, the preciousness of it, the miracle of it, the strength needed to bring it forth and the care needed to sustain it.

With a worried sigh, she forced her attention back to her work. She'd traced the Grand Cayman banker to a number of stateside businesses, but all of them were perfectly legitimate and had nothing to do with Fang Baolian. She doubted if the two of them were in league on anything other than the banker providing his professional services to a customer with an inordinate amount of cash.

The running of the fax machine brought her head around, and she pushed away from her desk to go over and see what was coming in. The first page was a hastily scrawled note: *Hello, luv—Tell Cooper he owes me another eight hundred pounds. Original sent by courier. George.*

The second page of the transmission was a photograph. At first glance, and despite the lack of clarity, Jessica thought it was a picture of Cao Bo, and she was a little irritated. The information wasn't worth eight hundred pounds. It wasn't worth two pounds. They already knew what Cao Bo looked like. What they needed to know was where she'd come from, who she represented, why in the world she'd searched Cooper out at exactly the right time with exactly the right information.

Bo had given them the world on a platter and asked for nothing except protection. George Leeds sent a useless photograph and asked for eight hundred pounds. No wonder Cooper's financial base was dissolving like so many sand castles in a deluge. His friends were a greedy lot.

Jessica picked up the picture when the transmission was finished and carried it back to her desk. Bo had once had much longer hair, she noted with interest, and wondered when the young woman had had herself shorn.

She stopped by her chair and rested her hand on its back, her gaze fastened on the photograph. After a moment's perusal, her brows drew together in bewilderment. Something about the nose wasn't quite right. She couldn't decide what was different, but something was. The same held true for the mouth, and the shape of the face. As a matter of fact, the longer she looked at the picture, the less it looked like Bo—yet the resemblance was much more than skin-deep. The quality of the smile, if not the smile itself, was an exact match. There was an indefinable similarity about the eyes of both women, and despite the difference in the length of their hair, their hairlines were carbon copies of each other. The same delicate widow's peak added a sense of drama to both faces. The same graceful curve outlined each face from brow to temple to ear.

Jessica suddenly knew whom she was looking at, and her hand started to tremble. She loosened her hold and stepped back, letting the photograph flutter to the floor.

From the balcony doorway, Cooper only saw the stricken expression on her face, and in three strides he was at her side.

"Jessie." He grasped her upper arms and pulled her around to face him. "What's wrong?"

She stared up at him, her eyes wide, her skin paler than normal. "We're in trouble, Cooper, big, huge, unbelievable trouble."

He absorbed the seriousness of her statement and came up with only one conclusion. "It's your fertile time of the month, isn't it," he said, resigned to the facts. If a man loved a woman, certain things came along with it. Personally, Cooper loved most of those things. Women had cycles, like the moon, and the tides, and seasons like the Earth herself. Women were so . . . so connected. "Well, we'll wait this out, and the next time we'll use industrial-strength condoms instead of just the regular ones."

He loved making her blush, really loved it.

"Cooper, I am not talking about babies," she sputtered. "At least not my babies, or your babies."

"Then whose babies are we talking about?" he asked in confusion.

"Fang Baolian's babies."

Jessica watched the news settle on him, then he shook his head in denial.

"Fang Baolian doesn't have any babies," he said.

"She's got one, Cooper, one about eighteen years old, five feet three inches tall, less than a hundred and five pounds soaking wet. Trust me."

"Cao Bo?" he asked, his face grim.

"Cao Bo."

His gaze locked on hers, and an unholy gleam came to life in his eyes, glittering green and ruthless. "I guess that gives us the point, the game, and the match."

"You can't hurt her, Cooper."

"No," he agreed, not sounding at all reliable. "But I can use her."

# FOURTEEN

Word had gone out, leaked through a hundred sources who had spread it through a thousand Southeast Asian waterways and alleys: The Dragon had captured the Dragon Lady's hatchling.

Ripples were immediately felt in Manila, where a customer ready to pay two hundred thousand dollars U.S. for a ship he'd picked out to be pirated in the Bay, was told the price had suddenly gone to three hundred thousand cash before delivery.

On the docks in Singapore, a shipment of motorcycles was hijacked after the owner had already paid protection money. In Jakarta, the financing for a new international resort, hotel, and convention complex was suddenly and inexplicably withdrawn.

Fang Baolian was consolidating her resources for war. Every dollar she squeezed out of the black market was proof of the worth of Cao Bo. Every dollar was an obstacle for Jessica to overcome.

Cooper had called in his favors from Seattle to

San Diego and Cabo San Lucas. The ports were being watched. The borders were being patrolled. He couldn't believe his luck.

He had been grinning for three days.

Jessica did not find the expression reassuring or pleasant, and she certainly did not find it humorous.

He'd offered her a bonus for working the weekend and staying on as a private consultant throughout the next week. She'd politely told him where he could put his bonus. She no longer wanted his money, originally the main impetus for her being in her present mess. She wanted him.

She looked up from her desk and checked the clock. Cooper had gone downtown hours ago. He'd been contacted by a man with information to sell on the Grand Cayman banker. She was supposed to meet him at the office before they went to dinner. After spending most of the day with her nose buried in numbers, transactions, and a host of foreign names, she was glad it was finally time for her to leave.

Despite the ocean view and the panoramic vistas, his home was beginning to feel like a prison with all the hours she'd spent in the makeshift office, especially with everyone else gone. Within minutes after Cooper had realized who Bo was, he'd decided to put her in hiding. Arrangements had been finalized in less than an hour, and John and Yuxi had taken her across the Bay.

Bo had shown little reluctance to go with them, partially, Jessica thought, because of John. He was the type of man who inspired confidence, and Bo seemed to have responded to him instinctively. Jessica had seen a number of shy glances pass from Bo to the quietly serious dark-haired warrior-houseboy. John had been more discreet, but no less interested. A fact proved by his choice of a safe house, an upscale suburban home in Oakland, where Bo would be chaperoned by his mother and sister, and protected by himself, Yuxi, and a brother trained in the ancient defensive arts of Shaolin monks.

No good could come of it, Jessica was certain, not any of it. Fang Baolian had murdered Jackson Daniels, and now her daughter was a willing hostage of the murdered man's brother. Not even John had been able to get Bo to explain why she'd given her mother's secrets to a man sure to use them against her.

The mystery didn't sit right, rife as it was with potential for unforeseen disaster. Cooper knew the dangers, but was pushing forward, undaunted, with his plan. Jessica hoped she wouldn't be left alone to pick up the pieces.

With a last glance at the clock, she pushed out of her chair and reached for her purse. A few papers slid off the desk when she failed to lift the purse clear of her workpile. She bent to retrieve the loose documents, and one of them caught her eye. It was the message she'd left Cooper the night he had returned from Hawaii, the one telling him about the aborted phone call and how worried she was about him.

Cooper hadn't made much of the call. He had dismissed it by saying it could have been any one of a hundred people he knew who were invariably down on their luck or in their cups, but it still bothered her.

She saw it as another loose end in a situation that was getting damn tangled up with loose ends.

There wasn't anything she could do about it that night. She had a dinner to eat and a noose to tighten. Locking up, she let herself out of the house.

Paul was baby-sitting and having an at-home date with the owner of a greenhouse. Jessica had promised herself and the children that she'd make up for all the time they'd missed in the last two weeks before she looked for another job. And she was determined to look for another job.

She refused to work for a man she was in love with, and she'd fallen in love with Cooper Daniels. At least that's what she was afraid had happened. She was mature enough to realize the emotional boundaries of her maternal instincts were broader than they should be, easily broad enough to include a man felled by grief, especially if that man was green-eyed, gorgeous, and made love like no one she'd ever heard about, let alone experienced.

She realized her lack of sexual experience with anyone other than Ian made her susceptible to overestimating the importance of the astounding physical pleasure Cooper gave her. And to over-romanticizing the profound emotional pleasure she felt when he held her afterward and whispered to her of his own satisfaction and his appreciation of her as his lover.

She'd never been anyone's lover before. She'd been Ian's wife and the mother of his children first and foremost. Their personal and family relationships had seemed perfectly normal to her at the time, a lot of give and a little take, with her being responsible for everyone's happiness except her own, because sacrificing herself was the noblest achievement a woman could aspire to.

In retrospect, her marriage looked like a bad movie, complete with an all-too-familiar and predictable ending, but only distance and time had given her that clearer perspective. She'd always considered herself liberated, unfettered by tradition. She'd had the best education money could buy and dedicated parents could provide. Her self-esteem had always been healthy. But thousands of years of male-dominated culture were hard to ignore, and she had ended up in a comfortable but dangerous rut of dependency, and the even stranger rut of being dependent upon her family's dependency on her.

The situation with Cooper was completely different. It was novel, and intriguing, and full of potential for heartbreak, but with little potential for dependency. It was difficult, if not downright impossible, to become dependent on a man who probably wouldn't live through the next week.

Damn him.

Even staying married to Ian for as long as she had looked smart compared with giving her heart to a bounty hunter.

The lights in the Daniels, Ltd. offices were on when Jessica made her first pass. By the time she found a parking place, they were off.

She peeked up through her windshield and tried hard not to be irritated. They were supposed to meet at the office. They'd agreed there was no reason for both of them to pay for the valet parking at the restaurant.

Her fingers idly tapped the steering wheel, and she expelled a heavy breath, waiting to see if he came out the front door, or if she'd missed him. One minute passed, then two, then three and four, and still he didn't show up. Five minutes seemed like a lifetime, six and seven were nearly unbearable, and by eight minutes her fingers were reaching for the ignition.

The front door opened, and her fingers stopped in midtwist. Cooper wasn't alone. Four men were with him, one in front and one in back, and one on each side of him, appearing to be holding him up, or restraining him.

The four men had a lot in common. They all wore dark slacks and light loose shirts without the tails tucked in. They all wore plain white tennis shoes— and they were all Chinese.

Fang Baolian had made her move.

Jessica forced herself to breathe and to think beyond the fear threatening to overwhelm her. She searched Cooper for signs of distress, and found enough to make her whole body stiffen with tension. He wasn't holding his head straight. His knees were bent, his legs not moving as fast as he was, proving he was being carried. They'd either drugged him or beaten him. Both possibilities filled her with a potent mixture of fear and rage.

They stuffed him into a waiting car, which pulled away from the curb with a squeal of tires almost before the last man's foot had left the sidewalk. The white sedan disappeared over the hill while Jessica was still fumbling with her keys. She didn't stop to think about what she was doing. She just reacted.

Tearing off with her own tires squealing, her compact caught some air on the first downslope, enough to scare the hell out of her and make her quickly reevaluate her priorities. She couldn't save Cooper if she totaled her car, and saving Cooper was her single, compelling priority. She wouldn't let him be hurt, not while there was a breath left in her body. The desperation she felt was palpable.

She held her car to the road, and when she spotted the white sedan up ahead of her, she slowed to a reasonable distance. She didn't have to follow the car for long. Three turns brought them into the heart of Chinatown, and two more blocks brought them to the herb shop on Grant Street. Any doubts she'd had about who had abducted Cooper dissipated.

After Baolian's photograph had come in, the herb shop had taken a backseat to other details. Now, Jessica would have given anything to have continued her research into it. She wished John Liu had come down and checked the layout of the store. She wished she had a car phone to call the San Francisco Police Department and a big brother or two.

She wished she could find a parking space. The white sedan had gotten away with double parking until its passengers were unloaded. While she was still inching along, praying for a miracle, it cruised off into the night.

Chinatown was alive with neon and exotic smells, and crowds of people searching out a bargain and a meal. All of them were in her way, frustrating her effort to see Cooper and the men dragging him down the street and into the alley running next to the herb shop. When she lost sight of him for more than fifteen seconds, she muttered a foul curse and threw the compact into its parking gear in the middle of the street. A horn honked behind her. She ignored it, concentrating her efforts on pulling her driver's license out of her wallet and jamming it into the clip on the driver's-side sun visor. With Signorelli listed as her middle name, it was a calling card guaranteed to get someone's attention down at headquarters.

She checked three of her doors to be sure they were locked before she pocketed her Magnum in her suit coat. Lights blinked and glowed in an abstract pattern of red-and-gold characters reflected in her windshield and on the hood of her car. Next to the Chinese characters the words were lit in blue and written in pinyin and English: ZHONGYI—CHINESE MEDICINE.

With her purse slung over her shoulder, she unsnapped her ring of keys from the one in the ignition, got out, and locked the driver's-side door. More honking greeted her traffic-jam stunt. She only hoped one of the irate drivers called the cops.

Cooper's arms were bound behind him and his legs had turned to rubber. Every time he tried to stand up or catch up, they refused to cooperate. He was having a hell of a time focusing too, and he knew his condition had a lot to do with a recent head wound. Very recent, like less than an hour old. Ditto for the nausea. Head wounds always made him nauseous.

He'd been royally shanghaied, and there wasn't a damn thing he could do about it except try to keep himself from getting killed. A niggling in his brain told him the survival trick was going to be harder to pull off than it had ever been before. He knew who had him, and he knew his luck had run out.

The smells on the street told him they were in Chinatown. A minute later the smells told him they were in a Chinatown alley. They were as distinct and unpleasant as those in any downtown alley, but with a fragrant backdrop of dim sum and moxibustion herbs sneaking through the rot and the garbage.

It took a few more minutes and the enveloping darkness of a narrow stairwell filled with a thousand scents of dried plants and the muskier smell of desiccated animal parts before he made the connection with the Grant Street herb shop.

Jessie had incredible instincts, he realized with more than a bit of admiration and awe. She'd been right about the shop and she'd been right about Cao Bo, and the two of them together were how she would finally be the death of him. Without her unerring intuition to guide him, he would have wandered through a labyrinth of possibilities without ever getting this close to getting himself killed.

He'd known a woman could succeed where a hundred men had failed. He'd counted on a woman being the key, staked his reputation and his last dime on a woman—and she'd been worth every penny, though the ironic relationship between her success and his demise wasn't lost on him.

The muted light at the bottom of the stairs spread and grew nominally brighter as they descended, until they reached the bottom and a room barred like a cell door. Inside, a wizened old man sat on a pile of shabby pillows, drawing on a pipe and watching the world through opium-glazed eyes. His queue was unbraided in places, with lank strands of gray hair sticking out at odd angles like a broken spiderweb against his black tunic. A pot of tea steamed on a low table next to the pillows.

The room was no bigger than six feet by six feet, paneled in teak and set with tarnished brass like the captain's quarters of a ill-kept ship, but Cooper could have imagined worse places to be incarcerated.

He was pushed down next to the old man, who gave him a toothless grin and blew smoke in his face. He tried to turn away, but there was no escaping the sickly-sweet smell.

Three of the guards came into the room and began stripping off their shirts while the fourth man disappeared back up the stairs. There were hooks along one wall, each holding a black tunic with a red insignia on the shoulder. Crates were stacked haphazardly against two of the other walls, along with various bolts of cloth and a few cases of Chinese and German beer.

The guards made quick work of changing into the tunics. No motions were wasted. They were all lean and muscled, hardened fighting men. Red headbands with a Chinese character brushstroked across the front were tied on last, completing their uniforms.

Their transformation did plenty to increase Cooper's apprehensions. He hadn't been kidnapped by just any old pirates. Fang Baolian's private honor guard had been sent to capture him.

The man Cooper guessed was in charge, because of the double insignia on his sleeve, spoke in Mandarin to the others, and the men laughed. The old man kept blowing smoke in his face, irritating him and adding to his lethargy at the same time, while the guards all had a beer and chattered much too quickly for him to follow the conversation.

Certain words did register on his pain-fogged brain. None of them eased his growing sense of doom.

One word was "ransom," which could have had a heartening effect, but the sum mentioned was beyond the resources of anyone who might care enough to pony up the price. It was a price calculated to aggrandize him, giving great honor to his captor, but it also ensured his inevitable death and inevitable loss of face when no one paid. In short, ransom was a lose-lose proposition for him.

The next few words he understood dealt mainly with different methods of killing, some so gruesome as to make him wish he was already dead. Closing his eyes for a moment, he rested his head on a bolt of silk and tried to force some clarity into his jumbled thoughts. The effort was almost beyond the stupor he was beginning to feel, though the old man's opium hadn't done enough damage to ease the pain lancing through him from the base of his skull to the small of his back, places where he'd been kicked, chopped, and punched. His lungs hurt with the effort to draw air, and when he lifted his lashes, he thought he might never get his eyes to focus, or his body to stop trembling—trembling like a leaf in a gale, he realized with a surge of panic. He was shaking from head to foot, or rather he was being shook.

He instinctively braced himself between the wall behind him and the case of beer beside him, but it was like trying to brace a cooked noodle. His body wouldn't cooperate with what little rationality he had left to work with. A distant rumbling, resonating as if it came from deep within the earth, grew in sound and power.

*Earthquake.*

And the big one, if Cooper knew anything about the rattling and rolling of good old Mother Nature. The other men in the room seemed remarkably unconcerned with the natural disaster preparing to engulf them. Then the shaking stopped with a loud thump.

One of the walls slid to the side, revealing a grate that the leader released and pushed up out of the way. The room was actually a freight elevator, and they'd just gone down, down past any possible sort of building basement. They were at the core of the Earth.

Cooper's mouth tightened at the sight of the abyss awaiting him outside the teak room. For a minute he wondered if he was still in San Francisco, or if he'd passed out somewhere between Powell Street and the airport and had been taken someplace far away.

An endless array of tunnels snaked out from the elevator, their differing directions marked only by faint smudges of light in the far-reaching darkness. If this was Chinatown, he was at the nerve center. If Fang Baolian had come for her daughter, she was waiting for him here.

The men pushed him forward into the far-left opening. He went without a struggle, because there was no way for him to fight and win—and because he was suddenly very curious about what he would find at the other end of the tunnel.

# FIFTEEN

Jessica stepped into the shop and into another world. Hundreds, if not thousands, of clay and glass jars lined shelf after dusty shelf in the store. The cases holding the shelves were tall and narrow, stacked together with barely enough room between for a person to squeeze through. The only open space in the room was the slightly wider alley leading from the front door to the back counter, where an elaborate brass-and-ivory abacus lay next to an ancient cash register. Long strings of glass beads covered two doorways behind the counter.

Adjusting her purse strap on her shoulder to hold the bag closer to her body, Jessica walked forward slowly, careful not to nudge or bump anything. Her gaze drifted over the many jars, noting the different stoppers of cork and rags, the occasional metal screw lid. Each jar had two labels, both neatly lettered, the first in Chinese characters and the other an English translation.

Some of the translations inside one locked case gave her a moment's pause and made her stomach lurch. She'd never thought of dried tiger penis as a medicinal ingredient. Never. Truth be told, she'd never thought of tiger penis at all, let alone dried and packaged for sale.

A quick perusal of the rest of the shelf indicated that she'd found the aphrodisiac section. There were any number of antlers and horns stacked on the shelves, most of them showing some wear where they'd been ground down. She refrained from reading the labels on the more disreputable, animal-part-looking packages, having already discerned what was in them and not actually caring to compare sizes and shapes.

Another case had a display of acupuncture needles, and behind the counter were shelves of books, all old looking, some bound in leather, some rolls of parchment tied with silk cords. A delicate scale for weights and measures sat next to the register, and beside the scale was a small box of papers.

There was no sign of human habitation, but Jessica knew this had to be the place where they'd brought Cooper. By lifting a hinged section of the counter, she let herself get back by the books and the two doors. Her decision of which door to take was a toss-up, until she heard the sound of an even and steady gait coming from the door on the left. Without hesitating, she took the door on the right.

Cooper had lost track of how many tunnel off-shoots they'd passed, though he'd done his damnedest to remember. Any chance he had of getting out alive would require being able to negotiate the maze of pathways carved out of earth and stone, pathways made even more labyrinthine by the multiple intersections with the city's electrical and sewer conduits.

He'd never seen anything like it. He'd never smelled anything like it.

He couldn't imagine that Fang Baolian, Empress of the South China Sea and Dragon Whore Supreme of the aforementioned piece of watery real estate, would leave her luxurious phantom ship to live in a god-rotting hole in the ground. He found it even more difficult to imagine the meticulous Chow Sheng mincing his way down these tunnels to do the dragon whore's bidding, his silk robes dragging in putrid water and his soft kid slippers sliding through scum.

Rats, lots of rats, scurried hither and yon, squeaking and scuffling. But the rats didn't bother him nearly as much as the indefinable creatures he heard slapping and slithering around in the fetid pools. Blind fish came to mind, yet the rising hairs on the back of his neck insisted on telling him that what he was hearing wasn't fish, but something more reptilian, something with bigger teeth, maybe something with coils and fangs and slimy skin, something deformed from its aboveground origins.

In among the slapping and the slithering, if he listened carefully, he could hear an occasional low, plaintive hiss, as if the creatures were in pain, or hungry.

His skin was crawling by the time they came to the end of a tunnel that did not branch off into another four directions. A door built like an air lock was set into stone, the only light being the red glow of an electronic keypad.

The leader of the guards stepped forward to key in the lock combination and turn the wheel. When the door opened with a whoosh, Cooper was pushed forward into a blinding light. His shoes were removed, and he was pushed forward once more, this time to his knees in front of a dais covered in rich folds of pearlized cream silk. The whole room was ornate with gold filigree and rosewood screens, and richly opulent Oriental rugs. The wool was softly alive beneath his hands and a welcome cushion for his knees, colored in shades of richest green to palest peach and cinnabar.

For a moment he was almost comfortable. The rug was beautiful, the air was sweet, no one was dragging him around. Paradise.

Without warning, his head was jerked back by a rough, skilled hand, sending a shaft of pain ricocheting down his spine. Another ounce of force or degree of angle and his neck would have been broken, snapped like a dry twig in a child's hands. He clenched his teeth to keep from crying out, though any cry would have been strangled in the unnatural arch of his throat.

"Koo-pare Dan-yells." A melodious voice, soft and seductive, slowly spoke his name, pronouncing each syllable with practiced precision.

He opened his eyes to that voice, to the lure in its sultry promise, in the huskiness of her tone, and what

he saw made him wonder what had kept his brother
from taking what she'd offered.

She was exquisite, utterly exquisite, beyond compare even with her daughter. Any sign of age was
solely in her strangely amber eyes. No flaw marred
the perfection of her pale skin. No lines broke the
porcelain serenity of her face. There was only beauty,
ethereal, mesmerizing beauty, rising out of the dais
like a black-sheathed calla lily.

The rounded swells of her breasts, the curves of
her hips, the slender length of her legs were all lov-
ingly encased in luminescent ebony silk. Her hair *was*
ebony silk, piled high on her head and held in place
with diamond-and-jet pins. Her mouth was made for
sex, her lips full and stained the color of pomegranate
juice to match her long, daggerlike nails.

Cooper felt a stirring in his loins and wondered if
he'd lost his mind as well as his control. Fang Baolian
was the woman who had murdered his brother. The
woman who had ordered his own death and failed.

Even as he went over the facts his eyes traveled
the length of her again, accepting that part of his
battle with her would be waged within himself. She
was dangerously erotic, enticing, a challenge to be
met and conquered in the most primal of male-female
arenas.

From her hiding place behind a carved openwork
screen, Jessica saw the glitter of lust in Cooper's eyes,
and she almost shot him on the spot. She'd practically
killed herself trying to find her way through a dis-
gusting maze of tunnels so she could save him, and

he was salivating over the little bitch in the black dress. The only thing that saved him was the trace of opium she sniffed in the air. He may have only been beaten before, but he was beaten and drugged now.

"I have waited overlong to meet the brother of Jack Sun," Baolian purred, and Jessica's hackles rose. The woman moved like a cat in heat, descending from the dais to curl around and rub against the man being held in a viselike grip.

Her long scarlet-tipped index fingernail scraped along Cooper's jaw, up his cheek, and into the sun-streaked silkiness of his hair, carefully avoiding the bloody gash Jessica saw at his temple.

"But now we have met, Koo-pare, and I would hope you would have a gift for me. A priceless gift."

Jessica had a gift for Ms. Fang. She'd wrapped it in the steel chamber of her Magnum.

Baolian's fingers trailed down behind his ear, and in the next instant Cooper was writhing on the floor, caught in the stranglehold of the Dragon Lady. Jessica saw the slight oozing of blood running from beneath Baolian's fingernails. The only explanation was nearly unbelievable. The woman's manicurist did razors.

"Where is she?" Baolian hissed. "You son of a dung-eating slut! Where is my daughter? Tell me or you shall die!"

Jessica had never heard a mother's love expressed quite so inelegantly, quite so succinctly, and she suddenly understood what had sent Cao Bo into the Dragon's den.

She had to make her move, before Baolian did something drastic, like cut his jugular. She had to make her move, but she couldn't get it out of her head that she was a mother, a woman with responsibilities, a woman who had to be careful.

"Damn," she whispered, well under her breath, but it was enough to make every set of eyes in the place bear down on her.

The only move left to her was to lift and cock her gun, and point it straight at the dragon whore's heart as she stepped from behind the screen.

"Put your hands up . . . bitch." It was corny and rude, but the command was also amazingly effective when backed up by a powerful handgun.

Baolian released Cooper and he dropped to the floor in a heap, but her hands rose no farther than to carefully clenched fists at her hips. The metallic slither of a switchblade being opened sounded in the room. Baolian warned the guard off with an acid glare and a low hiss—and every nerve ending Jessica had sizzled in alarm.

The sound wasn't quite human, and neither was the expression on Baolian's face. Her cold, hooded eyes raked Jessica from head to toe as if she were sizing up a meal. The woman was no cat. She was a snake, a reptile, a creature of dark power fueled by the light of love for her child.

The dragon whore glided forward, her eyes hypnotically fixated on Jessica's. Jessica tried to blink and couldn't. Her inability set off another round of distress signals in her brain. Fight-or-flight responses flared to life in an instant, and just as quickly collided in her muscles, derailing each other and leaving her helpless.

Baolian smiled, a sinister, seductive curve of redrimmed lips. With a flick of her wrist and a fanning of her fingers, she made the razor tips of her nails flash and wink in the light, sending a straight shot of terror through Jessica from the top of her bangs to the tips of her toes.

It was going to be a bloodbath.

"Hello, Dove," Baolian purred, raising her other hand and letting those tiny daggers fan out and shine. "You I did not expect today, or I would have prepared a more appropriate welcome."

Jessica's arm ached with holding the gun, but she didn't let it drop.

"Are you Jack Sun's Dove?" Baolian asked, gliding forward another foot. "Or are you Koo-pare's Dove? Which Dragon calls you master? The dead or the dying?"

Jessica was going to have to kill her. She was going to have to kill a woman, and she didn't know if she could.

"Must be Koo-pare's," Baolian seemed to decide on a whim. "Jack Sun did not like old women." Her smile turned sour and a malevolent light flickered in her eyes. "Jack Sun did not like this not-so-old woman, no? It is what caused his death, this aversion and other things. Foolish, foolish man.

"So, Dove, master of the dying Dragon, my child has been lost to me. Do you know where she is?"

It was a mother's plea from a viper's mouth. Jessica didn't answer.

Baolian's anger rose with every second of silence. "Do you know?" she asked again, tight-lipped. "Have you seen my Shulan? The child of my heart? If you know, you must tell me, or you will die. You all will die. *All*, Dove. *All*, Jessssss-ica Yangston."

The hiss and the emphasis wasn't lost on Jessica, neither was the use of her name, but the full meaning of Baolian's words didn't hit home until she spoke again.

"Which will be worse, do you think, Dove? A child, or maybe two, without their mother? Or a mother without her children?"

"The girl who came to the Dragon was called Cao Bo, not Shulan," Jessica said, her voice relaying the sudden deep and abiding calm she felt. Baolian had made a mistake by showing her hand and making her threat. If the situation deteriorated to the point of death, it would be Baolian's death, not Jessica's children's.

"Cao Bo?" Baolian scoffed. "Her name is Shulan, Sun Shulan, and she is a princess of the South China Sea. What I have built will be hers. She is my life. Give her to me, and I will give you and your children life."

It was an offer Jessica would have accepted, except for the man on the floor.

"What about Cooper?" she asked.

Baolian gave her a curious look. "You value a pet as you value your children?"

Pet? Jessica thought. Cooper was in trouble, big, deep, huge trouble. Thinking she was doing the right thing, she tried not to sound overly eager.

"He has value to me."

"More value than your children?"

The question was impossible, angering, and just about got the dragon whore shot.

"The question, Ms. Fang," Jessica said in her best Ms. MBA-from-Stanford voice, "is how much you value the return of *your* child. If you accept such as the basis of our discussion, fine. If not, if you continue to mistake that the discussion is about *my* children, I'm going to blow a hole in you big enough to float a hundred-and-twenty-thousand-ton tanker. And that, Ms. Fang, is one hell of a hole."

Baolain hissed halfheartedly and turned to ascend the dais. When she was seated on her throne, she gave Jessica a petulant look. "Tell me what you know."

The woman gave all the right signs of conceding defeat. The dismissal of the matter as if it weren't important, the childish expression, the more reasonable, less reptilian tone.

Jessica didn't buy the act for a minute.

"Shulan is being held across the Bay. When Cooper and I are safely out of here, and I have had a chance to call home, I will give you the address."

Baolian clapped her hands and spoke to one of the guards in Chinese. The dialect didn't sound like the Cantonese of Chow Sheng and John Liu. The guard came forward and from out of a silk-lined box brought forth an old-fashioned phone with a very long cord.

"Talk to your children," Baolian said, gesturing at the phone. "And then I will talk to mine."

It sounded like a fair plan to Jessica.

She dialed her home phone number, and Paul answered.

"Hi, Paul. It's Jessie," she said, amazed at how calm she still sounded. "Are the kids there?"

"Yes, they're here, and I just want to say what a wonderful time they're having on my date with the most gorgeous greenhouse owner in the whole Bay Area. I thought I had a pretty good chance with her, but then she met Eric, and he did something really goofy, like tell her how pretty she was, and now I think they're planning to get married after a long engagement."

Jessica attempted a short laugh, then wished she hadn't bothered when it came out like a croak. Her arm was shaking from the strain of holding the gun. Her mind was going a hundred miles an hour trying to keep up with watching three guards, one dragon lady, one hurt dragon man, and manage the most important conversation of her life.

"Can I speak with him, please. And get Christina on the other line."

"Sure, Jess," he said, the teasing humor going out of his voice. "Are you okay?"

"I'm fine, but come back on after the kids are finished."

The children came on then, and talked their little hearts out about the pizza Uncle Tony had made them for dinner, and about the neat lady who liked Uncle Paul, and when Mommy was coming home.

When her brother got back on, she didn't waste words. "I'm in trouble."

"Where?"

"Underneath Chinatown, and I'm sure that's all I can tell you." A nod from Baolian confirmed her suspicion.

Paul told her what he thought of that in one foul word. "What in the hell do you mean *underneath* Chinatown?"

"Underneath, as in not on top."

Baolian made a cutting motion across her throat, warning Jessica to say no more.

"Okay, okay," Paul said. "I believe you. You're underneath Chinatown. Fine. Great. Now tell me where underneath Chinatown. Give me a clue."

It was a great idea, really great, and she wished like hell she could think of a clue she could fit into the conversation without setting off Baolian and the three Ninja Turtles waiting to take her head off. But she couldn't.

"Don't let the children out of your sight. Call Luke. Luke *Signorelli* and do just like he says—shoot anybody who tries to cross the threshold and then drag them inside." It was the best clue she could come up with, emphasizing her maiden name and hoping somebody had called the cops about the crazy lady who had locked a double-parked car in front of an herb shop in Chinatown.

Anything Paul might have wanted to say was cut off by one of the guards disconnecting the phone from the wall. When he plugged it back in, Baolian gestured for her to make her second call.

"Why drag them inside?" she asked while Jessica tried to remember John Liu's phone number.

"We're in America. Criminals have rights." The number was on the tip of her memory bank, right on the tip.

"Maybe I'll move to America," Baolian mused aloud.

The look Jessica gave her said, "Maybe not."

She'd only called out to the Liu house a couple of times. But either fear or grace finally brought the number up in her mind.

"John? Jessie. Put Bo on the line."

"Hello?" the young woman said a moment later.

Jessica handed the phone over to Baolian, then was chagrined to realize the conversation between mother and daughter was not going to take place in English. She'd been curious about what a throat-cutting, dragon-whore, pirate mother had to say to a daughter who misbehaved.

Remarkably, the throat-cutting, dragon whore, pirate mother sounded a lot like herself, with an appropriate increase in the chastisement quality of her tone of voice, given the seriousness of the daughter's actions.

After a few minutes Baolian handed the phone back to Jessica. "Please speak with John Liu so that he doesn't get himself killed trying to keep my child from me."

It was a reasonable request, and Jessica complied.

"John. Cooper and I are in trouble, and it will go

a lot easier on us if you let Cao Bo, or rather Sun Shulan, go."

She got an argument, not much of one, but an argument she didn't have time for.

"Just a minute, John." She put her hand over the receiver and asked Baolian a question. "How old is Shulan?"

"Seventeen next week."

"John," Jessica went back on the line. "She's younger than she looks. Give her back to her mother."

The phone was taken from her and returned to its silken box. The tension in the room had dropped considerably, but Jessica still didn't have any idea of what would happen next, so she kept her gun trained on Baolian.

Cooper groaned, drawing her attention, and in that second she was disarmed by someone from behind.

Baolian smiled. "The only danger here today was for you and your pet," she said, acknowledging the man who had stepped out from behind the rosewood screen and taken Jessica's ninth wedding anniversary present out of her hands. "When Shulan is here, maybe you can take your dragon and go."

With a clap of her hands, the guards fell into action, picking Cooper up off the floor and grabbing Jessica.

Maybe? she thought, her mouth dry with fear. She struggled against the men holding her, but to no avail. She was caught, without the skills to take on three well-trained men.

Still, she didn't make it easy for them to drag her

out of the plush room and into the darkness of the maze. Cooper came to consciousness once, when a blast of cold air whirled up out of the tunnels and dropped the temperature by twenty degrees in a matter of seconds.

The guards spoke seldom, leaving only the labored breathing of six people and the sound of their footsteps to echo in the silent bowels of the Earth. The walls grew clammy about them, and the darkness deepened, until the only light left was from a lantern carried by one of the guards.

Timeless minutes later, most of it spent walking at a downhill slant, she and Cooper were thrown into a dank, fetid cell with no lantern of their own and only rats to keep them company.

Jessica shuddered from the cold and fear and snuggled closer to the man she was sure she was going to die with.

"Cooper?" Her teeth chattered around his name. She shook him. "Cooper?"

"Yes?" he said weakly.

She let out a squeal when something skittered around the edge of her shoe. "Can you get to your feet?" Her voice took on added urgency. "We need to get out of here. Now."

Cooper opened his eyes to nothing but darkness; he looked around and saw nothing but darkness. He felt like hell, like somebody had tied a noose around his neck, bruising him and rubbing him raw.

"Where are we, Jess?" he mumbled, not quite back with the living yet.

"I don't know, but if we can't find a way out, we're going to die, or be eaten by something."

Great, he thought.

"What . . . what kind of something?" he asked.

"I don't know—ahh!" She squealed again. "What was that? Did you feel that?"

"I'm pretty numb, Jess."

"I'm getting out of here." Her voice shook, and he wished like hell he was in better shape to help her.

He'd seen the way she'd fought for him, stood up for him when she'd had the chance to walk away. He didn't know how she'd found him, or why she'd followed him, but he knew he owed her his life.

"What?"

"What?" he asked back, confused.

"What was that noise you made?"

"I didn't make any noi—"

An eerie cry keened through the darkness, stunning them both into absolute paralysis. The wail rose to a high-pitched whine, growing louder before dropping off into a hiss.

Cooper cursed and broke into a cold sweat.

Jessica clung to him like he was the last log in the ocean, digging her nails into his forearm.

"It's an animal," she whispered, her voice strained through fear.

"I hope," he said curtly and without an ounce of confidence.

"It's an animal," she repeated. "I saw it on my way down."

"You *saw* it?"

"Sort of saw it," she amended. "It's in a cage in one of the tunnels. There wasn't much light."

"You saw that thing, and you kept coming?" His voice rose in disbelief and kept rising. "I thought I hired you for your *brains*, not to get yourself *killed*."

The cry came again, not quite so plaintive and more searching, as if the creature that made it had lifted its snout into the air to detect a trace of prey.

"Cooper?"

"Yes?" They were both whispering.

"I think it can hear us."

"I thought you said it was caged."

"It was . . . at least on one side."

A long stretch of silence fell between them.

"A cage with one side is not a cage, Jessie."

"I know."

He took her hand in his and slowly got them both to their feet. "But if it can get out, maybe we can too. From what little I remember from the first trip down, this place is riddled with tunnels. I doubt if there's a secure hole down here."

"You're right about the tunnels," she said. "They're everywhere and they always seem to run into each other."

He tightened his hold on her, giving her hand a squeeze. "Then it's time to take a chance, Jessie."

# SIXTEEN

"Ms. Langston. May I see you in my office, please?"

Jessica leaned forward and pressed the response panel on the intercom. "Yes, Mr. Daniels. I'll be right in."

She stopped and poured them both a cup of coffee before she breezed through the dragon doors and walked straight over the top of the dragon on the floor to his desk. The fierce beast with emerald eyes and fire dancing on its tongue had been tamed.

"Thanks, Jessie." Cooper took the coffee from her and handed her the morning paper. "It's been a week. I'm surprised we're still making the front page."

Jessica skimmed the *Chronicle*, finally finding an article toward the bottom with the dubious headline of PIRATE BUSTERS SHUT DOWN HERB SHOP. That's what she'd been reduced to, a pirate buster, she who had graduated at the top of her class.

"I think you're pretty well all washed up as far as

the financial district goes, honey," Cooper said, not doing a very good job of hiding his grin.

He was right. She'd become notorious practically overnight, when she'd dragged herself out of a Chinatown sewer and into the bright lights of a television crew filming the biggest traffic jam to hit Grant Street since the Chinese New Year. Four squad cars had been on the scene, with Luke Signorelli in the lead of a small platoon of cops looking for the lady who had locked her double-parked car and left it running.

When Cooper had hauled himself out behind her, he, too, had become an instant, if fleeting, celebrity. The media were more interested in a woman bounty hunter than a man. They especially liked that she was a single mother, a super mom, the woman who could do it all—work her sedate job as an investment counselor during the day, bust pirates by night, and tuck the children into bed in between.

They were wrong, of course. She had a brother who did kitchen work for a living. Her children never went hungry or had to settle for fish sticks, because they had an Uncle Tony whose idea of fast food was angelhair pasta. She had another brother who spent all of his free time at home, where he was always available to watch the kids, because the love of his life was finding the bifurcation points of the indigenous species in the yard.

She also had a boss who understood that after nearly a month of working for him, she needed an extended vacation. For a week now she'd come into the office just before lunch, allowed Mr. Daniels to wine her and dine her through the noontime meal, then had gone home to burn cookies for the kids after school.

She got to the end of the article and tossed the paper aside. "So the feds have closed down the shop pending further investigation, and they're tracing a lead to Grand Cayman. Baolian never surfaced, and we're assuming she sailed out the Golden Gate with her recalcitrant daughter in tow. Where does that leave us, Cooper? Did we win?"

"There was no way to win, Jess," he said, his smile fading into an expression that was part resignation, part acceptance. "But we did damn good."

"Where are we having lunch?" she asked, changing the subject. He was right. There had been no way to win, not from the moment his brother had died on a beach in the South China Sea. She was grateful he'd finally come to that understanding.

"Your choice," he said. "Better make it someplace nice. I think Daniels, Ltd. is going to be belly-up by the end of the year." He didn't sound too distressed by the possibility.

"Oh, I wouldn't go that far," she said, hiding her own grin. "I heard Mr. Daniels hired himself a really hot MBA out of Stanford who can make money just by reading the stock pages. With a little capital investment, the MBA could save the company."

"Maybe Mr. Daniels ought to take the MBA to lunch instead of the sweet lady he's been spending so much time with lately."

"Maybe." She smiled at him, and was surprised to see him blush. Damn surprised. "Cooper?"

He lowered his lashes, averting his gaze, and began fumbling through his leather coat pockets. "You saved my life, Jessie, and you know what they say, if somebody saves your life, you owe them a life."

"I've heard the expression, but really, Cooper, I'm not planning on getting into any more trouble."

"Yeah, well, none of us plans on getting into trouble. It just happens." He finally pulled a small box free of his coat. His blush deepened, fascinating her. "I've had to do a lot of thinking these last few days, and a lot of what I've been thinking about is you." He looked up at her. He was very beautiful, her dragon, with his emerald eyes and his sun-streaked hair. "Life is pretty damn tenuous, Jessie. I want you to have whatever is left of mine."

She accepted the box with trembling hands. "Better be careful, Cooper. A woman could take a statement like that a lot of different ways."

She opened the velvet-lined box and gasped. The ring inside was gaudy and outrageous. It was gold and big, with a dragon with emerald eyes and a dove with diamonds, locked in either mortal combat or a tender embrace. It said *By Love Alone* on the inside in a delicately engraved script.

"Take it however you want," he said. "Indecent proposal, or marriage proposal. For the kids' sake and mine, though, I'd rather you went for the legally binding contract."

Jessica brushed at the tears in her eyes, wondering

what always made women cry when they were happy. "I'm going for the legal partnership."

He slipped the ring on her finger, and she couldn't believe how wild it looked, or how much she loved it. Her conservative image was in serious danger.

"I love you, Jessie," he said, taking her hand in his and pulling her down onto his lap. "I'm giving you the ring to be my wife. I want you to know your love is safe with me."

Another wave of tears ran down her cheeks, and she brushed those away too.

"Is there a reason you're crying that I need to know about?" he asked.

She shook her head. "I'm crying because I'm so happy."

"Ah," he said, not sounding the least bit enlightened.

"I think you're going to have to kiss me, Cooper, to take my mind off how happy I am."

He didn't need a second request, but pulled her mouth down to his to softly plunder, taste, and tease, until her tears were replaced by passion.


"Cooper?" Jessica came up beside him on the deck of his house and put her arm around his waist. In front of them, the Pacific Ocean stretched all the way to the South China Sea and beyond.

Cooper pulled her to his side and bent down to kiss her lips. Some hurts might never heal, he mused, some people would never be replaced, but the awful emptiness he'd felt since Jackson's death was slowly being filled with love—Jessie's love with her motherly quirks, and all the wanton love she gave him in bed. The children liked him enough for a good relationship to grow, and he was fascinated by them. Christina was so delicate and strong, so like her mother. Eric's biggest disappointment was that the Dragon didn't have an actual dragon tattooed on his body somewhere. Cooper had told them there had once been a dragon with a tattoo. That dragon had been Jackson, and it was time to put his memory in a place of rest instead of a place of pain.

"This just arrived by courier," she said when the sweet kiss was over, holding up an ancient-looking envelope.

The chop set in wax on the back made his spine stiffen.

"What is it?" she asked.

"Baolian. It's her chop." He took the envelope and broke the seal, his moment of contentment gone. With quick movements, he snapped open the letter, not knowing what to expect, but somehow expecting something different than the few words she'd written.

He swore softly and handed the letter to Jessica. She read it aloud. "Shulan tells me I must tell you I am most sorry for Jack Sun. She says this will help us, all of us."

She folded the letter back into its envelope and set it on a deck chair. Then she took his hand in hers.

"Come on." She pulled him toward the bedroom.

"Are the kids asleep?" For her sake he forced a smile.

"Like a couple of rocks."

He wanted her, he always wanted her, but he couldn't hold the smile in place. "Jessie, I know what you're doing, but you can't make all the hurt go away with love."

She looked up at him, and what he saw in her eyes made a liar out of him.

"Oh, yes you can, Cooper. Love is an amazing thing."

He believed her enough to go with her, and it didn't take much faith to continue believing her while she was in his arms. By the time the deepest part of the night had fallen, he was a convert.

He woke later, restless, and eased out of bed, careful not to wake her. Fog had slipped in over the coast while they'd slept. The deck was a netherworld of muted sounds and skyless night. With a soft tread, he went back to where they'd stood and bent to pick the letter up off the chair where they'd left it. His fingers encountered only the wooden slats of the chair. The letter was gone, blown by the wind into the sea, where all earthly life had been created.

Cooper waited for the sense of loss to come, but the only thing that came to him was Jessie, to wrap her warmth around him.

# EPILOGUE

Sun Shulan stood in her house on the Peak, looking out a window that framed Victoria Harbor and the Hong Kong skyline. She'd done her best, and her best had not been good enough. Her mother still ruled the South China Sea, unchecked and unreformed; the half brother she'd risked her life to save was still in danger.

With a heavy sigh, she turned and forced herself too meet fiery emerald eyes of the man being held in the foyer by her guards. His hair flowed to his waist like a river of black silk. Powerful muscles strained beneath the coolie clothes she'd bought for him to wear.

Holding him captive was like trying to cage a wildcat . . . or a dragon. She couldn't do it forever, couldn't hide him forever, and yet his only protection was that Baolian thought Jackson Daniels, Sun Yi's bastard son, was dead.

Another sigh escaped her as she turned back toward the window. Someday she would have to let him go.

Someday soon.

# THE EDITOR'S CORNER

Next month, LOVESWEPT is proud to present **CONQUERING HEROES,** six men who know what they want and won't stop until they get it. Just when summer is really heating up, our six wonderful romances sizzle with bold seduction and daring promises of passion. You'll meet the heroes of your wildest fantasies who will risk everything in pursuit of the women they desire, and like our heroines, you'll learn that surrender comes easily when love conquers all.

The ever-popular Leanne Banks gives us the story of another member of the Pendleton family in **PLAYING WITH DYNAMITE,** LOVESWEPT #696. Brick Pendleton is stunned when Lisa Ransom makes love to him like a wild woman, then sends him away! He cares for her as he never has another woman, but he just can't give her the promise that she insists is her dearest dream. Lisa tries to forget him, ignore him, but he's gotten under her skin, claiming her with every caress of his mouth and hands. The fierce demolition expert knows everything about tearing things down, but rebuilding Lisa's trust means fighting old demons—and confessing fear. **PLAYING WITH DYNAMITE** is another explosive winner from Leanne.

**CAPTAIN'S ORDERS**, LOVESWEPT #697, is the newest sizzling romance from Susan Connell, with a hero you'll be more than happy to obey. When marina captain Rick Parrish gets home from vacation, the last thing he expects to find is his favorite hang-out turned into a fancy restaurant by Bryn Madison. The willowy redhead redesigning her grandfather's bar infuriates him with her plan to sell the jukebox and get rid of the parrot, but she stirs long-forgotten needs and touches him in dark and lonely places. Fascinated by the arrogant and impossibly handsome man who fights to hide the passion inside him, Bryn aches to unleash it. This determined angel has the power to heal his sorrow and capture his soul, but Rick has to face his ghosts before he can make her his forever. This heart-stopping romance is what you've come to expect from Susan Connell.

It's another powerful story of triumph from Judy Gill in **LOVING VOICES**, LOVESWEPT #698. Ken Ransom considers his life over, cursing the accident that has taken his sight, but when a velvety angel voice on the telephone entices him to listen and talk, he feels like a man again—and aches to know the woman whose warmth has lit a fire in his soul. Ingrid Bjornson makes him laugh, and makes him long to stroke her until she moans with pleasure, but he needs to persuade her to meet him face-to-face. Ingrid fears revealing her own lonely secret to the man whose courage is greater than her own, but he dares her to be reckless, to let him court her, cherish her, and awaken her deepest yearnings. Ken can't believe he's found the woman destined to fill his heart just when he has nothing to offer her, but now they must confront the pain that has drawn them together. Judy Gill will have you laughing and crying with this terrific love story.

Linda Warren invites you to get **DOWN AND DIRTY**, LOVESWEPT #699. When Jack Gibraltar refuses to help archeology professor Catherine Moore find her missing aunt, he doesn't expect her to trespass on his turf, looking for information in the seedy Mexican bar! He admires her persistence, but she is going to ruin a perfectly good con if she keeps asking questions . . . not to mention drive him crazy wondering what she'll taste like when he kisses her. When they are forced to play lovers to elude their pursuers, they pretend it's only a game—until he claims her mouth with sweet, savage need. Now she has to show her sexy outlaw that loving him is the adventure she craves most. **DOWN AND DIRTY** is Linda Warren at her best.

Jan Hudson's conquering hero is **ONE TOUGH TEXAN**, LOVESWEPT #700. Need Chisholm doesn't think his day could possibly get worse, but when a nearly naked woman appears in the doorway of his Ace in the Hole saloon, he cheers right up! On a scale of one to ten, Kate Miller is a twenty, with hair the color of a dark palomino and eyes that hold secrets worth uncovering, but before he can court her, he has to keep her from running away! With his rakish eye patch and desperado mustache, Need looks tough, dangerous, and utterly masculine, but Kate has never met a man who makes her feel safer—or wilder. Unwilling to endanger the man she loves, yet desperate to stop hiding from her shadowy past, she must find a way to trust the hero who'll follow her anywhere. **ONE TOUGH TEXAN** is vintage Jan Hudson.

And last, but never least, is **A BABY FOR DAISY**, LOVESWEPT #701, from Fayrene Preston. When Daisy Huntington suggests they make a baby together, Ben McGuire gazes at her with enough intensity to strip the varnish from the nightclub bar! Regretting her impulsive words almost immediately, Daisy wonders if the man might just be worth the challenge. But when she finds an abandoned baby in her car minutes later, then quickly realizes that several dangerous men are searching for the child, Ben becomes her only hope for escape! Something in his cool gray eyes makes her trust him—and the electricity between them is too delicious to deny. He wants her from the moment he sees her, hungers to touch her everywhere, but he has to convince her that what they have will endure. Fayrene has done it again with a romance you'll never forget.

Happy reading,

With warmest wishes,

*Nita Taublib*

Nita Taublib
Associate Publisher

P.S. There are exciting things happening here at Loveswept! Stay tuned for our gorgeous new look starting with our August 1994 books—on sale in July. More details to come next month.

P.P.S. Don't miss the exciting women's novels from Bantam that are coming your way in July—**MISTRESS** is the newest hardcover from *New York Times* best-selling author Amanda Quick; **WILDEST DREAMS,** by best-selling author Rosanne Bittner, is the epic, romantic saga of a young beauty and a rugged ex-soldier with the courage to face hardship and deprivation for the sake of their dreams; **DANGEROUS TO LOVE,** by award-winning Elizabeth Thornton, is a spectacular historical romance brimming with passion, humor, and adventure; **AMAZON LILY,** by Theresa Weir, is the classic love story in the best-selling tradition of *Romancing the Stone* that sizzles with passionate romance and adventure as deadly as the uncharted heart of the Amazon. We'll be giving you a sneak peek at these terrific books in next month's LOVESWEPTs. And immediately following this page look for a preview of the exciting romances from Bantam that are *available now*!

Don't miss these extraordinary books by your favorite Bantam authors

On sale in May:

# DARK JOURNEY
*by Sandra Canfield*

# SOMETHING BORROWED, SOMETHING BLUE
*by Jillian Karr*

# THE MOON RIDER
*by Virginia Lynn*

"A master storyteller of stunning
intensity."
—*Romantic Times*

# DARK JOURNEY
## by Sandra Canfield

*From the day Anna Ramey moved to Cook's Bay, Maine,
with her dying husband—to the end of the summer when
she discovers the price of forbidden passion in another
man's arms, DARK JOURNEY is nothing less than
electrifying.* Affaire de Coeur *has already praised it as
"emotionally moving and thoroughly fascinating," and*
Rendezvous *calls it "A masterful work."*

*Here is a look at this powerful novel . . .*

"Jack and I haven't been lovers for years," Anna
said, unable to believe she was being so frank. She'd
never made this admission to anyone before. She
blamed the numbness, which in part was culpable,
but she also knew that the man sitting beside her
had a way of making her want to share her thoughts
and feelings.

Her statement in no way surprised Sloan. He'd
suspected Jack's impotence was the reason there
had been no houseful of children. He further suspected that the topic of discussion had something
to do with what was troubling Anna, but he let her
find her own way of telling him that.

"As time went on, I adjusted to that fact," Anna
said finally. She thought of her lonely bed and of

more lonely nights than she could count, and added, "One adjusts to what one has to."

Again Sloan said nothing, though he could painfully imagine the price she'd paid.

"I learned to live with celibacy," Anna said. "What I couldn't learn to live with was . . ."

Her voice faltered. The numbness that had claimed her partially receded, allowing a glimpse of her earlier anger to return.

Sloan saw the flash of anger. She was feeling, which was far healthier than not feeling, but again she was paying a dear price.

"What couldn't you live with, Anna?"

The query came so softly, so sweetly, that Anna had no choice but to respond. But, then, it would have taken little persuasion, for she wanted—no, needed!—to tell this man just how much she was hurting.

"All I wanted was an occasional touch, a hug, someone to hold my hand, some contact!" She had willed her voice to sound normal, but the anger had a will of its own. On some level she acknowledged that the anger felt good. "He won't touch me, and he won't let me touch him!"

Though a part of Sloan wanted to deck Jack Ramey for his insensitivity, another part of him understood. How could a man remember what it was like to make love to this woman, then touch her knowing that the touch must be limited because of his incapability?

"I reached for his hand, and he pulled it away." Anna's voice thickened. "Even when I begged him, he wouldn't let me touch him."

Sloan heard the hurt, the desolation of spirit, that lay behind her anger. No matter the circum-

stances, he couldn't imagine any man not responding to this woman's need. He couldn't imagine any
man having the option. He himself had spent the
better part of the morning trying to forget the gentle touch of her hand, and here she was pleading
with her husband for what he—Sloan—would die
to give her.

A part of Anna wanted to show Sloan the note
crumpled in her pants pocket, but another part
couldn't bring herself to do it. She couldn't believe
that Jack was serious about wishing for death. He
was depressed. Nothing more.

"What can I do to ease your pain?" Sloan asked,
again so softly that his voice, like a log-fed fire,
warmed Anna.

*Take my hand.* The words whispered in Anna's
head, in her heart. They seemed as natural as the
currents, the tides of the ocean, yet they shouldn't
have.

*Let me take your hand,* Sloan thought, admitting
that maybe his pain would be eased by that act. For
pain was exactly what he felt at being near her and
not being able to touch her. Dear God, when had
touching her become so important? Ever since that
morning's silken memories, came the reply.

*What would he do if I took his hand?*

*What would she do if I took her hand?*

The questions didn't wait for answers. As though
each had no say in the matter, as though it had been
ordained from the start, Sloan reached for Anna's
hand even as she reached for his.

A hundred recognitions scrambled through two
minds: warmth, Anna's softness, Sloan's strength,
the smallness of Anna's hand, the largeness of
Sloan's, the way Anna's fingers entwined with his

as though clinging to him for dear life, the way Sloan's fingers tightened about hers as though he'd fight to the death to defend her.

What would it feel like to thread his fingers through her golden hair?

What would it feel like to palm his stubble-shaded cheek?

What would it feel like to trace the delicate curve of her neck?

What would it feel like to graze his lips with her fingertips?

Innocently, guiltily, Sloan's gaze met Anna's. They stared—at each other, at the truth boldly staring back at them.

With her wedding band glinting an ugly accusation, Anna slowly pulled her hand from Sloan's. She said nothing, though her fractured breath spoke volumes.

Sloan's breath was no steadier when he said, "I swear I never meant for this to happen."

Anna stood, Sloan stood, the world spun wildly. Anna took a step backward as though by doing so she could outdistance what she was feeling.

Sloan saw flight in her eyes. "Anna, wait. Let's talk."

But Anna didn't. She took another step, then another, and then, after one last look in Sloan's eyes, she turned and raced from the beach.

"Anna, please . . . Anna . . . *Ann-nna!*"

# SOMETHING BORROWED, SOMETHING BLUE
by
# Jillian Karr

When the "Comtesse" Monique D'Arcy decides to
feature four special weddings on the pages of her
floundering *Perfect Bride* magazine, the brides find
themselves on a collision course of violent passions
and dangerous desires.

*The T.V. movie rights for this stunning novel have
already been optioned to CBS.*

The intercom buzzed, braying intrusively into
the early morning silence of the office.

Standing by the window, looking down at the sea
of umbrellas bobbing far below, Monique D'Arcy
took another sip of her coffee, ignoring the insistent
drone, her secretary's attempt to draw her into the
formal start of this workday. Not yet, Linda. The
Sinutab hasn't kicked in. What the hell could be so
important at seven-thirty in the morning?

She closed her eyes and pressed the coffee
mug into the hollow between her brows, letting
the warmth seep into her aching sinuses. The
intercom buzzed on, relentless, five staccato blasts

that reverberated through Monique's head like a jackhammer.

"Dammit."

She tossed the fat, just-published June issue of *Perfect Bride* and a stack of next month's galleys aside to unearth the intercom buried somewhere on her marble desk. She pressed the button resignedly. "You win, Linda. What's up?"

"Hurricane warning."

"*What?*" Monique spun back toward the window and scanned the dull pewter skyline marred with rain clouds. Manhattan was getting soaked in a May downpour and her window shimmered with delicate crystal droplets, but no wind buffeted the panes. "Linda, what are you talking . . ."

"Shanna Ives," Linda hissed. "She's on her way up. Thought you'd like to know."

Adrenaline pumped into her brain, surging past the sinus headache as Monique dove into her fight or flee mode. She started pacing, her Maud Frizon heels digging into the plush vanilla carpet. Shanna was the last person in the world she wanted to tangle with this morning. She was still trying to come to grips with the June issue, with all that had happened. As she set the mug down amid the organized clutter of her desk, she realized her hands were shaking. Get a grip. Don't let that bitch get the better of you. *Oh, God, this is the last thing I need today.*

Her glance fell on the radiant faces of the three brides smiling out at her from the open pages of the magazine, faces that had haunted her since she'd found the first copies of the June issue in a box beside her desk a scant half hour earlier.

Grief tore at her. Oh, God, only three of us. There were supposed to have been four. There *should* have been four. Her heart cried out for the one who was missing.

This had all been her idea. Four stunning brides, the weddings of the year, showcased in dazzling style. Save the magazine, save my ass, make Richard happy. All of us famed celebrities—except for one.

Teri. She smiled, thinking of the first time she'd met the pretty little manicurist who'd been so peculiarly reluctant at first to be thrust into the limelight. Most women dreamed of the Cinderella chance she'd been offered, yet Teri had recoiled from it. *But I made it impossible for her to refuse. I never guessed where it would lead, or what it would do to her life.*

And Ana, Hollywood's darling, with that riot of red curls framing a delicate face, exuding sexy abandon. Monique had found Ana perhaps the most vulnerable and private of them all. *Poor, beautiful Ana, with her sad, ugly secrets—I never dreamed anyone could have as much to hide as I do.*

And then there was Eve—lovely, tigerish Eve, Monique's closest friend in the world, the once-lanky, unsure teenage beauty she had discovered and catapulted to international supermodel fame. *All I asked was one little favor . . .*

And me, Monique reflected with a bittersweet smile, staring at her own glamorous image alongside the other two brides. Unconsciously, she twisted the two-and-a-half-carat diamond on her finger. Monique D'Arcy, the Comtesse de Chevalier. *If only they knew the truth.*

Shanna Ives would be bursting through her door any minute, breathing fire. But Monique couldn't stop thinking about the three women whose lives had become so bound up with her own during the past months. Teri, Ana, Eve—all on the brink of living happily ever after with the men they loved . . .

For one of them the dream had turned into a nightmare. *You never know what life will spring on you*, Monique thought, sinking into her chair as the rain pelted more fiercely against the window. *You just never know. Not one of us could have guessed what would happen.*

She hadn't, that long-ago dawn when she'd first conceived the plan for salvaging the magazine, her job, and her future with Richard. Her brilliant plan. She'd had no idea of what she was getting all of them into. . . .

# *THE MOON RIDER*

## by VIRGINIA LYNN

bestselling author of
**IN A ROGUE'S ARMS**

"Lynn's novels shine with lively adventures,
a special brand of humor
and sizzling romance."
—*Romantic Times*

*When a notorious highwayman accosted Rhianna and her father on a lonely country road, the evening ended in tragedy. Now, desperate for the funds to care for her bedridden father, Rhianna has hit upon an ingenious scheme: she too will take up a sword—and let the heartless highwayman take the blame for her robberies. But in the blackness of the night the Moon Rider waits, and soon this reckless beauty will find herself at his mercy, in his arms, and in the thrall of his raging passion.*

"Stand and deliver," she heard the highwayman say as the coach door was jerked open. Rhianna gasped at the stark white apparition.

Keswick had not exaggerated. The highwayman was swathed in white from head to foot, and she thought at once of the childhood tales of ghosts that had made her shiver with delicious dread.

There was nothing delicious about this apparition.

A silk mask of snow-white was over his face, dark eyes seeming to burn like banked fires beneath the material. Only his mouth was partially visible, and he was repeating the order to stand and deliver. He stepped closer to the coach, his voice rough and impatient.

Llewellyn leaned forward into the light, and the masked highwayman checked his forward movement.

"We have no valuables," her father said boldly. Lantern light glittered along the slender length of the cane sword he held in one hand. "I demand that you go your own way and leave us in peace."

"Don't be a fool," the Moon Rider said harshly. "Put away your weapon, sir."

"I have never yielded to a coward, and only cowards hide behind a mask, you bloody knave." He gave a thrust of his sword. There was a loud clang of metal and the whisk of steel on steel before Llewellyn's sword went flying through the air.

For a moment, Rhianna thought the highwayman intended to run her father through with his drawn sword. Then he lowered it slightly. She studied him, trying to fix his image in her mind so that she could describe him to the sheriff.

A pistol was tucked into the belt he wore around a long coat of white wool. The night wind tugged at a cape billowing behind him. Boots of white leather fit him to the knee, and his snug breeches were streaked with mud. He should have been a laughable figure, but he exuded such fierce menace that Rhianna could find no jest in what she'd earlier thought an amusing hoax.

"Give me one reason why I should not kill you on the spot," the Moon Rider said softly.

Rhianna shivered. "Please sir—" Her voice quivered and she paused to steady it. "Please—my father means no harm. Let us pass."

"One must pay the toll to pass this road tonight, my lovely lady." He stepped closer, and Rhianna was reminded of the restless prowl of a panther she'd once seen. "What have you to pay me?"

Despite her father's angry growl, Rhianna quickly unfastened her pearl necklace and held it out. "This. Take it and go. It's all of worth that I have, little though it is."

The Moon Rider laughed softly. "Ah, you underestimate yourself, my lady fair." He reached out and took the necklace from her gloved hand, then grasped her fingers. When her father moved suddenly, he was checked by the pistol cocked and aimed at him.

"Do not be hasty, my friend," the highwayman mocked. "A blast of ball and powder is much messier than the clean slice of a sword. Rest easy. I do not intend to debauch your daughter." He pulled her slightly closer. "Though she is a very tempting morsel, I must admit."

"You swine," Llewellyn choked out. Rhianna was alarmed at his high color. She tugged her hand free of the Moon Rider's grasp.

"You have what you wanted, now go and leave us in peace," she said firmly. For a moment, she thought he would grab her again, but he stepped back.

"My thanks for the necklace."

"Take it to hell with you," Llewellyn snarled. Rhianna put a restraining hand on his arm. The Moon Rider only laughed, however, and reached out for his horse.

Rhianna's eyes widened. She hadn't noticed the horse, but now she saw that it was a magnificent Arabian. Sleek and muscled, the pure white beast was as superb an animal as she'd ever seen and she couldn't help a soft exclamation of admiration.

"Oh! He's beautiful. . . ."

The Moon Rider swung into his saddle and glanced back at her. "I salute your perception, my fair lady."

Rhianna watched, her fear fading as the highwayman swung his horse around and pounded off into the shadows. He was a vivid contrast to the darker shapes of trees and bushes, easily seen until he crested the hill. Then, to her amazement, with the full moon silvering the ground and making it almost shimmer with light, he seemed to vanish. She blinked. It couldn't be. He was a man, not a ghost.

One of the footmen gave a whimper of pure fear. She ignored it as she stared at the crest of the hill, waiting for she didn't know what.

Then she saw him, a faint outline barely visible. He'd paused and was looking back at the coach. Several heartbeats thudded past, then he was gone again, and she couldn't recall later if he'd actually ridden away or somehow just faded into nothing.

And don't miss these fabulous romances from Bantam Books, on sale in June:

## MISTRESS
Available in hardcover
by *The New York Times* bestselling author
**Amanda Quick**
"Amanda Quick is one of the most versatile and talented authors of the last decade."
—*Romantic Times*

## WILDEST DREAMS
by the nationally bestselling author
**Rosanne Bittner**
"This author writes a great adventurous love story that you'll put on your 'keeper' shelf."
—*Heartland Critiques*

## DANGEROUS TO LOVE
by the highly acclaimed
**Elizabeth Thornton**
"A major, major talent . . . a superstar."
—*Romantic Times*

## AMAZON LILY
by the incomparable
**Theresa Weir**
"Theresa Weir's writing is poignant, passionate and powerful."
—*New York Times*
bestselling author Jayne Ann Krentz

# OFFICIAL RULES

To enter the sweepstakes below carefully follow all instructions found elsewhere in this offer.

The **Winners Classic** will award prizes with the following approximate maximum values: 1 Grand Prize: $26,500 (or $25,000 cash alternate); 1 First Prize: $3,000; 5 Second Prizes: $400 each; 35 Third Prizes: $100 each; 1,000 Fourth Prizes: $7.50 each. Total maximum retail value of Winners Classic Sweepstakes is $42,500. Some presentations of this sweepstakes may contain individual entry numbers corresponding to one or more of the aforementioned prize levels. To determine the Winners, individual entry numbers will first be compared with the winning numbers preselected by computer. For winning numbers not returned, prizes will be awarded in random drawings from among all eligible entries received. Prize choices may be offered at various levels. If a winner chooses an automobile prize, all license and registration fees, taxes, destination charges and, other expenses not offered herein are the responsibility of the winner. If a winner chooses a trip, travel must be complete within one year from the time the prize is awarded. Minors must be accompanied by an adult. Travel companion(s) must also sign release of liability. Trips are subject to space and departure availability. Certain black-out dates may apply.

The following applies to the sweepstakes named above:

**No purchase necessary.** You can also enter the sweepstakes by sending your name and address to: P.O. Box 508, Gibbstown, N.J. 08027. Mail each entry separately. Sweepstakes begins 6/1/93. Entries must be received by 12/30/94. Not responsible for lost, late, damaged, misdirected, illegible or postage due mail. Mechanically reproduced entries are not eligible. All entries become property of the sponsor and will not be returned.

**Prize Selection/Validations:** Selection of winners will be conducted no later than 5:00 PM on January 28, 1995, by an independent judging organization whose decisions are final. Random drawings will be held at 1211 Avenue of the Americas, New York, N.Y. 10036. Entrants need not be present to win. Odds of winning are determined by total number of entries received. Circulation of this sweepstakes is estimated not to exceed 200 million. All prizes are guaranteed to be awarded and delivered to winners. Winners will be notified by mail and may be required to complete an affidavit of eligibility and release of liability which must be returned within 14 days of date on notification or alternate winners will be selected in a random drawing. Any prize notification letter or any prize returned to a participating sponsor, Bantam Doubleday Dell Publishing Group, Inc., its participating divisions or subsidiaries, or the independent judging organization as undeliverable will be awarded to an alternate winner. Prizes are not transferable. No substitution for prizes except as offered or as may be necessary due to unavailability, in which case a prize of equal or greater value will be awarded. Prizes will be awarded approximately 90 days after the drawing. All taxes are the sole responsibility of the winners. Entry constitutes permission (except where prohibited by law) to use winners' names, hometowns, and likenesses for publicity purposes without further or other compensation. Prizes won by minors will be awarded in the name of parent or legal guardian.

**Participation:** Sweepstakes open to residents of the United States and Canada, except for the province of Quebec. Sweepstakes sponsored by Bantam Doubleday Dell Publishing Group, Inc., (BDD), 1540 Broadway, New York, NY 10036. Versions of this sweepstakes with different graphics and prize choices will be offered in conjunction with various solicitations or promotions by different subsidiaries and divisions of BDD. Where applicable, winners will have their choice of any prize offered at level won. Employees of BDD, its divisions, subsidiaries, advertising agencies, independent judging organization, and their immediate family members are not eligible.

Canadian residents, in order to win, must first correctly answer a time limited arithmetical skill testing question. Void in Puerto Rico, Quebec and wherever prohibited or restricted by law. Subject to all federal, state, local and provincial laws and regulations. For a list of major prize winners (available after 1/29/95): send a self-addressed, stamped envelope entirely separate from your entry to: Sweepstakes Winners, P.O. Box 517, Gibbstown, NJ 08027. Requests must be received by 12/30/94. DO NOT SEND ANY OTHER CORRESPONDENCE TO THIS P.O. BOX.